STENDHAL

Armance

STENDHAL

Armance

OR, SCENES
FROM A PARISIAN SALON
IN 1827

TRANSLATED BY
Gilbert and Suzanne Sale

The Merlin Press
LONDON

© THE MERLIN PRESS LTD. 1960
112 WHITFIELD STREET LONDON W.1

MADE AND PRINTED IN GREAT BRITAIN BY
CHARLES BIRCHALL & SONS LTD.
LONDON AND LIVERPOOL

FOREWORD

A woman of intelligence, who has no very fixed ideas upon literary merit, has begged me, unworthy as I am, to edit the style of this novel. I am far from sharing certain political views which seem to run through the narrative; this is what I wanted to tell the reader. Upon a great many subjects the charming author's thoughts and mine are poles apart, but we both have an equal horror of what are called *applications*. Very pointed novels are being written in London : *Vivian Grey, Almak's High Life, Matilda,* etc., which require a key. They are amusing caricatures directed against people whom the hazard of birth or fortune has placed in an enviable position.

This is a kind of literary merit which we do not seek at all. The author has not since 1814 been up to the first floor of the Palais des Tuileries; she has such pride that she does not even know the names of those persons who no doubt attract notice in certain circles.

But she has depicted and satirized manufacturers and members of the privileged class. If one were to ask the turtledoves for information about the Jardin des Tuileries, as they sighed in the summits of the tall trees, they would say : "It is an immense plain of greenery where we enjoy the brightest light." We, as strollers, would reply : "It is a delightful, shady place for a walk, where one is sheltered from the heat and particularly from the devastating daylight in summer".

Thus it is that each judges the same thing from his own point of view; *equally respectable* people who wish to follow different roads in order to lead us to happiness talk of the present state of society in just such conflicting terms. But each

5

heaps ridicule upon the other side.

Will you ascribe to an unkind twist in the author's mind the spiteful mendacity with which each party describes the salons of the opposition? Do you insist that passionate characters shall be wise philosophers—in other words that they shall have no passions? In 1760 one required graciousness, intelligence, and not too much temper nor too much honour—as the Regent said—in order to win the favour of the master and the mistress.

It needs good management, stubborn effort, reliability and a mind quite free of illusion, in order to make a success of the steam engine. Here is the difference between the century which came to an end in 1789 and that which began about 1815.

Napoleon, on his way to Russia, was for ever humming these words which he had heard so finely spoken by Porto (in *La Molinara*):

> *Si batte nel mio cuore*
> *L'inchiostro e la farina**

This is something that might well be repeated by many young people who are both well-born and intelligent.

In speaking of our own century, we find that we have sketched in outline two of the major characters of this Novelette. Possibly no more than twenty of its pages are in the least danger of seeming satiric; but the author has taken a different line; but the century is cheerless and irritable, and one must take certain precautions when dealing with it, even when publishing a booklet which, as I have already told the author, will be forgotten in six months at the latest, like the best of its kind.

In the meantime, we crave a little of the indulgence which has been shown to the authors of the comedy *Les Trois Quartiers*. They held a mirror to the public; is it their fault if ugly people passed in front of the mirror? To what party does a mirror belong?

* Shall I be a miller, shall I be a notary?

6

In the style of this novel will be found certain naïvetés of expression, which I have not had the courage to alter. Nothing is more tedious to me than Germanic, Romantic grandiloquence. The author was wont to say : "Too much striving after noble turns of phrase in the end leads to deference and to dryness; they encourage the reading of a page with pleasure, but such *dulcet preciosity* makes people shut the book at the end of the chapter, and we want them to read goodness knows how many chapters; so allow me my rustic or bourgeois simplicity."

Mind you, the author would be in despair if I were to believe her style *bourgeois*. There is an infinity of proud spirit in that heart of hers. It is the heart of a woman who would think herself older by ten years if her name were known. Besides, a subject such as this . . . !

STENDHAL

Saint-Gingouf, 23rd July 1827

CHAPTER I

It is old and plain
. . . It is silly sooth
And dallies with the innocence of love.
Twelfth Night, Act II

OCTAVE WAS barely twenty when he left the Ecole Poly-technique. His father, the Marquis de Malivert, expressed the wish that his only son should remain in Paris. Once Octave had satisfied himself that this was indeed the firm desire of a father whom he respected and of his mother whom he loved with something akin to passion, he gave up his plans to enter the Artillery. He would have liked to spend a few years with a regiment and then to have resigned his commission until the next war, in which he was equally prepared to serve as a lieutenant or as a colonel. This was one example of the peculiarities which made him hateful to men of common clay.

His keen wits, his tall stature and noble behaviour, his very beautiful large dark eyes would have earned Octave his place among the most distinguished young men in society, had not some shadow in those gentle eyes moved one to pity rather than envy. If he had felt a desire to talk he would have made a great sensation, but Octave had no desires; nothing seemed to cause him either pain or pleasure. As a child he had very often been ill, and it had been observed that since recovering his health and strength he always devoted himself unhesitatingly to what he considered the dictates of duty; but it might have been said

9

that without the call of duty he would have had no motive for action. Perhaps some strange principle deeply ingrained in his young heart, finding itself in conflict with the events of real life as he saw them unfolding around him, led him to picture against too sombre a background both his own future and his relationships with mankind. Whatever the cause of his deep melancholy, Octave seemed a misanthropist before his time. The Commandeur de Soubirane his uncle said one day in his presence that he was frightened by such a character.

"Why should I display myself other than as I am?" replied Octave coldly. "Your nephew will always tread the path of reason."

"But never on this side nor beyond it," rejoined the Commandeur with his Provençal vivacity; "from which I conclude that if you are not the Messiah awaited by the Hebrews you must be Lucifer in person, come back to this earth on purpose to plague my old bones. What the devil are you? I can't fathom you at all; you're the very *incarnation* of duty!"

"How happy I should be if I were never to fail in that!" said Octave; "how I wish I could return my soul to its Creator as pure as when He gave it me!"

"Marvellous!" cried the Commandeur. "There's the first time for a whole year that I've heard a wish expressed by a soul so pure that it's quite frozen!" And highly satisfied with this remark the Commandeur trotted out of the drawing-room.

Octave looked tenderly at his mother; she knew whether or not his soul was frozen. Of Mme Malivert it might be said that she had stayed young even though she was nearing fifty. This was not only because she was still beautiful but because with her extremely original and piquant mind she had retained a lively and obliging sympathy with the interests of her friends, and even with the misfortunes and joys of young people. She shared naturally in their reasons for hoping and fearing, and herself quickly seemed to hope or fear. Such a disposition has less grace now that public opinion apparently insists upon it as good form

10

for those women of a certain age who are not devout, but Mme de Malivert was untouched by affectation.

Her staff had observed for some time that she would leave the house in a cab, and that often, when she returned, she was not alone. Saint-Jean, an inquisitive old manservant who had been with his masters when they were *emigrés*, was curious to know the identity of a man whom Mme de Malivert had several times brought home. On the first day Saint-Jean lost sight of the stranger in a crowd; at the second attempt the fellow's curiosity met with greater success. He saw the man he was following enter La Charité hospital, and learned from the porter that the stranger was the celebrated Dr. Duquerrel. Mme de Malivert's staff discovered that their mistress was bringing home in succession all the most famous doctors in Paris and that she almost always found an opportunity for them to see her son.

Struck by the peculiarities she observed in Octave, she was afraid he might have a chest complaint. But she thought that if she were unfortunate enough to have guessed correctly, to mention the cruel disease would be to hasten its progress. Doctors, intelligent men, told Mme de Malivert that her son was suffering from no other disease than that kind of dissatisfied and censorious sadness characteristic of the young men of his time and rank; but they warned her that she herself should take the greatest care of her chest. This dire news spread through the household because of a diet which had to be followed, and M. de Malivert, despite the vain efforts of those who sought to hide the name of the disease from him, foresaw the possibility of a solitary old age.

Thoroughly dunder-headed and very rich before the Revolution, the Marquis de Malivert had returned to France only in 1814 in the wake of the king, to find his fortunes reduced by confiscation to twenty or thirty thousand francs a year. He considered himself a beggar. The one idea now in his head, which had never been particularly well-filled, was to see

11

Octave married. But with a regard for honour even greater than the ruling passion which tormented him, the old Marquis de Malivert invariably prefaced his overtures in society with these words : "I can offer a fine name, with an *unimpeachable* pedigree dating back to the Crusade of Louis the Young, and I only know thirteen families in Paris who can honourably make such a claim; but apart from that I find myself reduced to poverty, to taking alms. I'm a pauper."

This attitude in an elderly man is not calculated to induce that gentle, philosophical resignation which is the gladness of old age; and had it not been for the sallies of the old Commandeur de Soubirane, a slightly mad and rather malicious southerner, the house where Octave dwelt would have been remarkable for its gloom even in the Faubourg Saint-Germain.

Mme de Malivert, whom nothing could divert from her anxieties about her son's health—not even her own perils— seized the opportunity afforded by her weak condition, and cultivated the society of two famous doctors. She wished to gain their friendship. Since one of the gentlemen in question was the leader, and the other a most fervent supporter of two rival schools of thought, their discussions, albeit upon a subject so depressing for anyone not inspired by an interest in science and in the problem to be solved, sometimes amused Mme de Malivert, who had preserved a lively and inquiring mind. She encouraged them to talk, and thanks to them, at least, from time to time, a voice spoke out loud in the nobly-furnished but gloomy drawing room of the Malivert house.

A green velvet arras, overburdened with gilded decoration, seemed to have been made on purpose to absorb all the light that could be admitted by two huge windows fitted with mirrors instead of panes. These windows gave on to a secluded garden divided into peculiar compartments by box hedges. At the bottom stood a row of lime-trees, regularly trimmed thrice a year, whose motionless shapes seemed a living symbol of the way the family lived. The young Vicomte's room, which had been fitted in above the drawing-room, and sacrificed to the beauty of that essential part of the house, was barely higher than a mezzanine. Octave had a horror of the room, and had sung its praises a score of times in the presence of his parents. He feared lest some involuntary exclamation might betray him and show how profoundly he loathed that room and the whole house.

He bitterly regretted the loss of his little study at the Ecole Polytechnique. His years at the Ecole had meant a great deal to him, because they gave him a sense of the seclusion and peace of a monastery. For a long time Octave had intended to withdraw from the world and dedicate his life to God. The idea had alarmed his parents, particularly the Marquis, to whom it seemed the culmination of his fears of loneliness in old age. But in seeking to improve his knowledge of religious truths Octave had been led to the study of those writers who in the last two centuries have attempted to explain how man thinks and how he exercises his will; and his outlook had changed greatly, while that of his father had not. A passion for books in a young man of gentle birth the Marquis viewed with a kind of horror; he was for ever afraid the boy might relapse, and this was one of his chief motives in desiring Octave's prompt marriage.

It was while they were enjoying the last fine days of autumn, which in Paris is the spring, that Mme de Malivert said to her son: "You ought to go riding." All Octave could see in this suggestion was added expense, and as the continual complaints of his father led him to believe the family fortunes far slenderer than they really were, he refused for some time. "Why should I, mother?" he would invariably reply. "I can ride perfectly well, but I don't enjoy it at all." Mme de Malivert had a superb English horse placed in the stable, a horse whose youth and grace contrasted strangely with the two old Norman horses which for the last twelve years had served the needs of the household. Octave was embarrassed by this gift; he continued to thank his mother for two days, but on the third, finding himself alone with her, and when the topic of the English horse was raised : "I love you too much to thank you any more," he said, taking Mme de Malivert's hand and pressing it to his lips; "must your son for once in his life be insincere with her whom he loves best in all the world? That horse is worth four thousand francs, and you're not rich enough to afford an expense like that without inconvenience."

Mme de Malivert opened the drawer of a bureau. "Here is my will," she said. "I was leaving you my diamonds, but on one express condition, that as long as the proceeds of their sale lasted you were to keep a horse, which on my instructions you were occasionally to ride. I have had two of the diamonds secretly sold so that I may know the happiness of seeing you own a fine horse during my lifetime. One of the greatest sacrifices your father has imposed on me is to forbid me to dispose of these jewels so little suited to me. He has goodness knows what political aspirations—ill-founded in my opinion—and would think himself twice as poor and twice as ruined the day his wife no longer possessed her diamonds."

A look of profound sadness clouded Octave's brow, and he replaced in the bureau drawer the document whose name recalled so cruel and perhaps so imminent an occurrence. He took his mother's hand again and held it between his own, a gesture he rarely permitted himself.

"Your father's plans," continued Mme de Malivert, "depend on this law of indemnity we have been hearing about for the last three years."

"I hope with all my heart that it will be rejected," said Octave.

"And why?" enquired his mother, delighted to see him animated about something and giving her this proof of his esteem and friendship, "why would you like to see it rejected?"

"First because it's incomplete, and therefore unjust in my opinion, and second because it will lead to my marrying. It is

14

my misfortune to have a strange character, but this is not of my own making; all I have been able to achieve is self-knowledge. Except in those moments when I enjoy the happiness of being alone with you my only pleasure is to live in isolation, where not a soul in all the world has a right to speak to me."

"Octave, my dear, this singular taste springs from your immoderate passion for the sciences. Your studies really make me tremble; you'll finish up like Goethe's Faust. Are you prepared to swear to me as you did on Sunday that your reading does not consist solely of very wicked books?"

"I have read the works you have suggested for me, mother, at the same time as those you call wicked books."

"Oh, your character has something mysterious and sombre about it that makes me shiver; God knows what conclusions you draw from so much reading!"

"Mother dear, I can't refuse to believe what appears to me to be true. Could a good and almighty being punish me for giving credence to the evidence of the organs with which he himself has endowed me?"

"Ah, I'm always afraid of rousing the anger of that terrible being," said Mme de Malivert with tears in her eyes; "he has the power to wrest you from my love. There are days when reading Bourdaloue chills me with terror. I see in the Bible that this almighty being is ruthless in his vengeance, and you doubt-less offend him when you read the eighteenth century philo-sophers. The day before yesterday I came out of St. Thomas Aquinas's in a state honestly bordering on despair. Even if the Almighty's wrath against impious books is only a tenth of what M. l'Abbé Fay ✳✳✳ makes it out to be, I should still tremble lest I lose you. There's a dreadful newspaper which M. l'Abbé Fay ✳✳✳ did not even dare to name in his sermon, and which you read every day, I feel sure."

"Yes, mother, I do read it, but I keep the promise I made you; immediately afterwards I read the paper whose doctrine is exactly the opposite."

"Octave, my dear, it's the violence of your passions that alarms me, and above all the secret paths they follow in your heart. If only I could see in you one or two of the tastes suitable to your age, to take your mind off your strange ideas, I should be less afraid. But you read impious books, and soon you'll come to doubt the very existence of God. Why ponder over these terrible things? Do you remember your passion for chemistry? For eighteen months you wished to see no one; you offended our nearest relatives by your absence; you neglected the most essential duties."

"My taste for chemistry," replied Octave, "was not a passion, it was a task I set myself; and God knows," he added with a sigh, "whether it wouldn't have been better to remain faithful to my plan and to have become a scholar withdrawn from the world!"

That night Octave stayed with his mother until one o'clock. In vain she had urged him to venture into society, or at least to the theatre. "I stay where I am happiest," said Octave.

"There are times when I believe you," replied his mother, pleased, "when I am with you; but if for two days I have only seen you in the presence of others, reason regains the upper hand. That kind of solitude can't possibly be right for a man of your age. I have seventy-four thousand francs' worth of diamonds there, all useless, and likely to be so for a long time since you don't wish to marry yet; and in fact you're very young still—twenty years and five days!" And Mme de Malivert got up from her couch to give her son a kiss. "I have a good mind to sell these useless diamonds; I shall invest the money and use the interest to increase my expenditure; I should arrange an at-home, and on the excuse of my poor health I should invite absolutely no one except those to whom you have no objection."

"Alas, mother dearest, the sight of all men makes me equally sad; I love no one but you in the world. . . ."

After her son had left her, Mme de Malivert, disturbed by

16

sinister forebodings, could not get to sleep, despite the late hour. She tried vainly to forget how dear Octave was to her, and to judge him as she would have judged a stranger. Instead of following a line of reasoning her mind persisted in losing itself among romantic suppositions about her son's future; she recalled the Commandeur's remark. "Certainly," she said, "I feel something superhuman in him; he lives like a being apart, separate from other men." Bringing herself back later to a more reasonable approach, Mme de Malivert found it incomprehensible that her son should have the keenest or at least the most exalted passions and yet be so lacking in a taste for all the real things in life. It was as though his passions had their source elsewhere, and drew upon nothing here on earth. Everything about him, even his noble features, alarmed his mother; his beautiful, gentle eyes inspired her with terror. Sometimes they seemed to scan the heavens and to reflect the happiness they saw there. A moment later they were filled with the torment of hell.

One feels a certain reluctance to question someone whose happiness appears to be so fragile, and his mother used to watch him far more than she dared speak to him. In his calmer moments Octave's eyes seemed to be brooding over an absent happiness, as though a sensitive soul were far removed from something uniquely dear to it. Octave would reply sincerely to his mother's questions, yet she was unable to penetrate the mystery of that profound and often troubled reverie. Octave had been like this since the age of fifteen, and Mme de Malivert had never seriously considered the possibility of some secret passion. Was he not master of himself and of his fortune?

She was always noticing that real life, far from being a source of emotion for her son, merely irritated him, as if he were distracted by it and snatched annoyingly away from his beloved reverie. Though conceding how unfortunate was this way of life which seemed alien to all that surrounded her, Mme de Malivert could not help recognising that Octave possessed a

17

strong, upright soul, full of genius and honour. But this soul was well aware of its rights to independence and liberty, and its noble qualities were strangely allied with a capacity for pretence unbelievable at that age. In an instant this cruel reality came and shattered all the dreams of happiness which had soothed Mme de Malivert's imagination.

Nothing was more annoying to her son—one might even say more hateful, since he could neither love nor hate by halves —than the society of his uncle the Commandeur; and yet the whole household believed that he liked nothing better than to play chess with M. de Soubirane or to go 'dawdling' with him along the boulevards. The word was the Commandeur's; despite his sixty years he had at least as many pretensions as in 1789, save that empty argument and fatuous profundity had replaced the affectations of youth which at least had for excuse its graces and gaiety. This instance of easy dissimulation frightened Mme de Malivert. "I have questioned my son about the pleasure he takes in being with his uncle, and he has told me the truth, but who knows," she thought, "What strange plans may be hidden in the depths of that extraordinary soul? And if I never ask him about this, he'll never think of speaking to me of it himself. I am only a woman," Mme de Malivert told herself, "and am enlightened only about a few little duties within my grasp. How could I dare think myself fit to give counsel to so strong and so strange a being? I have no sufficiently clever friend to consult; besides, that would be to break Octave's confidence, and haven't I promised him absolute secrecy?"

When these dismal thoughts had tormented her till daybreak Mme de Malivert concluded as usual that she must use all her influence with her son to persuade him to go frequently and visit Mme la Marquise de Bonnivet. The latter was her cousin and intimate friend, a most highly respected woman whose *salon* was often the meeting-place of the most distinguished members of high society. "My own task," said Mme de Malivert to herself, "must be to cultivate these people of merit whom I meet at Mme de Bonnivet's, and so to find out what they think of Octave." Mme de Bonnivet's *salon* was frequented by those who sought both the pleasure of belonging to her circle, and the support of her husband, an able courtier advanced in years and in honours, who was almost as much in favour with his master as the genial Admiral de Bonnivet his ancestor, who caused François I to do so many stupid things, and punished himself so nobly for it.*

---

* At the battle of Pavia, towards evening, seeing that all was lost, the Admiral cried : "Never let it be said that I survived a disaster such as this," and raising his visor he leapt forward among his enemies, of whom he had the consolation of killing several before being cut down himself by repeated swordthrusts (24th February 1525).

CHAPTER II

Melancholy mark'd him for her own,
whose ambitious heart overrates the
happiness he cannot enjoy.

Marlowe.

THE FOLLOWING morning, from eight o'clock onwards, a great upheaval took place in Mme de Malivert's household. All the bells suddenly began to ring. Shortly afterwards the old Marquis was announced in his wife's room where she was still abed; he himself had not taken the time to dress. He came and kissed her with tears in his eyes: "My dearest," he said, "we shall see our grandchildren before we die," and the good old man wept hot tears. "Heaven knows," he added, "that it's not the thought of ceasing to be a pauper which has put me in such a state ... The law of indemnity is a certainty, and you'll have two million." At that moment Octave, who had been sent for by the Marquis, asked leave to come in; his father rose to his feet and embraced him roundly. Octave became aware of tears, and perhaps misunderstood their cause, for an almost imperceptible flush spread across his pale cheeks.

"Open the curtains wide; let in the daylight!" cried his mother animatedly. "Come here and look at me," she continued in the same tone, and without replying to her husband she examined the faint colour which had appeared over Octave's cheekbones. She knew from her discussions with the doctors that a red patch of colour on the cheeks is a symptom

20

of diseases of the chest; she was overcome with fear for her son's health and had no further thought for the two million franc indemnity.

At length, when Mme de Malivert was reassured, the Marquis, somewhat impatient at all this fuss, said : "Yes, my boy, I have just heard for certain that the law of indemnity is to be tabled, and we can rely on 319 votes out of 420. Your mother lost an estate which I calculate was worth more than six million, and whatever sacrifices the king's justice may be forced to make through fear of the Jacobins, we should be able to count on at least two million. So I'm no longer a pauper, which is to say that you're no longer a pauper; your fortune will now once again be in keeping with your birth, and I can now seek a suitable match for you without having to beg for it."

"Take care, my dear," said Mme de Malivert, "that your haste to believe this great news does not lay you open to the little remarks of our relative Mme la Duchesse d'Ancre and her circle. She herself actually enjoys all these millions you're promising us; don't count your chickens too soon."

The old Marquis pulled out his watch. "It's already twenty-five minutes," he said, "since I became certain, yes, positively *certain*, that the law of indemnity will be passed."

The Marquis must have been right, for that evening when the *impassive* Octave put in an appearance at Mme de Bonnivet's, he sensed a shade of eagerness in the welcome he received from everyone. There was also a shade of hauteur in his response to this sudden interest; at least the aged Duchesse d'Ancre remarked upon it. Octave's reaction was one of annoyance and contempt together. He saw that, *because of his expectations of two million*, he was more warmly received in Parisian society and among the people with whom he was on the most intimate terms. His ardent soul, as exacting and almost as stern towards others as towards himself, ended by deriving a profound sense of melancholy from this sad truth. It was not that Octave's hauteur stooped so low as to hold it against the people who chanced to be present in the drawing-room; he pitied his lot and that of all mankind. "So I am so little liked," he thought to himself, "that two million francs can change all their feelings for me; instead of seeking to merit their friendship I should have tried to grow rich in some business." While he was occupied with these dismal thoughts Octave was sitting on a divan, directly opposite a little chair occupied by his cousin, Armance de Zohiloff, and he happened to look at her. He noticed that she had not spoken to him all evening. Armance was a niece of Mme de Bonnivet and Mme de Malivert, almost without fortune, and about the same age as Octave; and as there was no more than indifference between them the two young people were in the habit of talking to each other with the utmost frankness. For three quarters of an hour Octave's heart had been brimfull of bitterness; suddenly it occurred to him that Armance had paid him no compliments, that she alone there was not a party to the redoubling of attentions which he owed to the money, that she alone there had some nobility of soul. And he found consolation in watching Armance. "There sits someone worthy of esteem," he thought, and observed, with a pleasure equal to the grief which had earlier filled his heart, that she continued not to speak to him.

Only once did Octave catch Armance glancing at him, just as a provincial member of the Chambre des Deputés was paying him a clumsy compliment upon the two million which *he was going to vote him* (these were the fellow's very words). It was impossible to mistake the meaning in this glance; at least Octave, with his unimaginable severity, chose to think so; the glance was intended to observe him; moreover—and this afforded him considerable pleasure—the glance was expected to have been contemptuous. The Deputé who was preparing to vote him two million fell victim to Octave; the young Vicomte's contempt was too patent even for a provincial. "That's the way they all behave," said the Deputé for the département of * * *

22

to the Commandeur de Soubirane whom he joined a moment later. "Ah, you gentlemen of the court nobility, if we could vote for our own indemnities without passing yours, by heaven, you wouldn't touch a sou until you had given us guarantees! We don't want to see you as before, colonels at twenty-three while we are captains at forty. Out of three hundred and nineteen right-thinking Deputés two hundred and twelve of us belong to the provincial nobility which was sacrificed in the past. . . ." The Commandeur, highly flattered at finding himself the recipient of such a complaint, fell to justifying people of quality. This conversation, which M. de Soubirane's self-importance styled as political, lasted all evening, and despite a piercing North wind betook itself into the recess of a window, the obligatory place in which to talk politics.

The Commandeur left it only for a moment, begging the Deputé to excuse him and await his return. "I must just ask my nephew what he's done with my carriage;" and he came and whispered to Octave: "Do some talking; your silence is being noticed; you mustn't become haughty just because of the new fortune. Remember those two million are a restitution and nothing more. Whatever would you do if the king had given you the Cordon Bleu?" And the Commandeur returned to the window recess, running like a young man, and repeating half-aloud : "Ah yes, the horses at half past eleven."

Octave began to talk, and if he did not achieve the ease and cheerfulness of manner which make for perfect social success, at least his remarkable beauty and air of deep earnestness caused many of the women to place a special value on the words he spoke to them. His ideas were lively and clear, and the more one considered them the greater they became. Certainly the noble simplicity with which he expressed himself robbed him of the effect of a few barbed sallies; only a second afterwards was one surprised. His natural hauteur never allowed him to emphasize what he considered a pretty remark. He was one of those people who by their pride are placed in the position of the

23

young woman arriving unrouged in a drawing-room where the use of rouge is the rule; for a few moments her pallor makes her appear sad. If Octave was a success it was because the high spirits and animation which he often lacked were replaced that evening by a sense of the bitterest irony.

Because of this caustic manner of his, women of a certain age were ready to forgive him his unsophisticated behaviour, and the fools whom he overawed hastened to applaud him. By subtly expressing all the contempt which consumed him, Octave was eliciting from society the only happiness it could give him, when the Duchesse d'Ancre came over near the divan where he sat; speaking not to him but for his benefit, she said in an undertone to her intimate friend Mme de la Ronze : "Look at that little fool Armance; I do believe she is jealous of the fortune which has fallen from the sky into M. de Malivert's lap? Heavens, how ill envy becomes a woman!" Her crony perceived the intent of the Duchesse, and took note of Octave's fixed stare; Octave, apparently engrossed in the venerable features of the bishop of *** who was speaking to him at the time, heard every word. In less than three minutes the silence of Mlle Zohiloff was explained, and she herself stood convicted, in Octave's mind, of all the base feelings with which she had just been charged. "Good God," he thought, "so there is not one exception to the baseness of all this group of people! And what grounds have I for thinking that other groups are different from this one? If they dare advertise such a devotion to money in one of the most select salons in France, where no one can open a history book without finding a hero who bears his name, what must it be like among miserable tradesmen millionaires today, but only a generation removed from mere pedlars? God, how vile men are!"

Octave fled from Mme de Bonnivet's drawing-room; society was detestable to him; he left the family carriage to his uncle the Commandeur and walked home. It was pouring, and he welcomed the rain. Soon he ceased to notice the minor tempest which was soaking Paris at that moment. The only recourse against this general degradation, he thought, would be to find a woman with a fine soul, not yet depraved by the so-called wisdom of people like the Duchesse d'Ancre; to cleave to this woman for ever, to see no one but her, to live with her and only for her and for her happiness. "I should love her passionately ... Love her! *I!* —unfortunate wretch that I am!" At that moment a carriage driven at the gallop out of the Rue de Poitiers into the Rue de Bourbon all but ran him down. The rear wheel dealt him a heavy blow in the chest, and tore his waistcoat. He stood stock-still; the encounter with death had cooled his blood.

"God, why was I not annihilated?" he said, looking up at the sky. And the torrential downpour did not make him lower his head; its coolness did him good. Only several minutes later did he walk on. He ran up to his room, changed his clothes, and enquired if he might see his mother. As she had not been expecting him she had gone early to bed. Alone with himself he found everything irritating, even the sombre Alfieri, one of whose tragedies he attempted to read. For a long time he paced up and down his vast, low-ceilinged room. "Why not have done with it all?" he asked himself at last; "why this obstinate struggle against the fate which overwhelms me? Whatever apparently reasonable plans I work out for my life, my existence is nothing but a succession of misfortunes and bitter sensations. This month is no better than last month, and this year no better than another; whence comes this obstinate insistence upon living? Can it be that I lack resolution? What is death?" he thought to himself, opening the case which contained his pistols, and looking at them. "Very little, in truth; it's madness to abstain from it. My mother, poor thing, is dying of consumption; in a very little time I shall have to follow her. And if life is too bitter a suffering for me to bear, I could go before her, too. If one could ask permission for such a thing, she would grant it me. The Commandeur now—even my

25

father—they don't love me; they love the name I bear; what they cherish in me is a pretext for their ambition. It's a very slender tie of duty which binds me to them...." The word *duty* struck him like a thunderbolt. "A *slender duty*!" he cried, pulling up short, "a trivial duty...! Can it be trivial if it is the only one I have left? If I don't overcome the difficulties which chance places in my way at this point, what right have I to dare believe myself so certain to surmount all those which may occur in the future? What, am I then arrogant enough to think myself superior to all dangers, to every kind of evil that may attack a man, and yet here am I begging the suffering which has befallen me to take a new form, to choose an aspect which suits me, in other words to halve itself. How paltry! And I thought myself so strong! I was giving myself airs!"

This new approach, and the making of a pledge to overcome the pain of living, were simultaneous. Soon the disgust which Octave felt for all things became less violent, and he himself felt less wretched. His soul, weighed down and disordered to some degree by so long a lack of all happiness, revived a little and took courage as he resumed his self-esteem. He began to entertain ideas of another kind. The squat ceiling of his room was anathema to him; he envied the Bonnivet house its magnificent drawing-room. "It must be at least twenty feet high," he calculated; "how comfortably I could breathe under that!" He continued suddenly with the gay surprise of a child: "Aha! Now there's a use for those millions! I shall have a drawing-room as magnificent as the one at the Bonnivets', and no one but I shall enter it. Every month, or—let me see—yes, on the first of every month a servant can dust it out, but under my supervision; I won't have him trying to guess my thoughts by my choice of books, or coming upon what I write to guide my soul in its moments of madness.... I shall always carry the key on my watch-chain, an infinitesimal one smaller than a wallet key. I shall have three mirrors in there, each seven feet high. I've always liked that kind of sombre, magnificent decoration. I wonder what the measurements are of the largest mirror they make at Saint-Gobain." And the man who for three quarters of an hour had been thinking of taking his own life promptly climbed on to a chair to hunt in his bookshelves for the Saint-Gobain mirror catalogue. He spent an hour writing out an estimate of the cost of his drawing-room. He realised that he was being childish, but only wrote the faster and the more earnestly. Having finished this task and checked the total which showed that it would cost 57,350 francs to install the drawing-room by raising the ceiling of his bedroom, Octave laughed to himself. "Well, if that's not counting my chickens before they're hatched . . . how ridiculous! Very well, I'm unhappy," he continued, striding up and down, "I'm unhappy, but I shall be stronger than my unhappiness. I shall measure myself against it, and I shall be the greater. Brutus sacrificed his children; that was the difficulty he had to face; as for me, I shall continue to live." He wrote in a little notebook hidden in the secret drawer of his desk: 14*th December* 182* : *Pleasant effect of two m.—Redoubling of friendship.— Envy in Ar.—End.—I shall be greater than it is.—Saint-Gobain mirrors.*

This bitter memorandum was entered in Greek characters. Next he played a whole act of *Don Giovanni* on his piano, and the dark chords of Mozart brought back peace to his soul.

CHAPTER III

As the most forward bud
Is eaten by the canker ere it blow,
Even so by love the young and tender wit
Is turn'd to folly . . .
. . . So eating love
Inhabits in the finest wits of all.
Two Gentlemen of Verona, Act I

IT WAS not always at night and alone that Octave was possessed by these crises of despair. At such times all his actions were coloured by an extreme violence, an extraordinary malevolence, and doubtless if he had been no more than a poor law-student, without relatives or protection, he would have been shut up as a madman. But again, in such a social position, he would not have had the opportunity to acquire that elegance of manner which, lending polish to so strange a character, marked him out as an individual apart, even in court society. The set of his features accounted in some measure for this extreme distinction in Octave; they were strong and gentle, and not at all strong and hard as is the case among the common run of men handsome enough to attract notice. He had a natural gift for the difficult art of communicating his thoughts, whatever they were, without ever giving offence, or at least without ever being needlessly offensive, and thanks to this perfect control in the ordinary relationships of life, the notion of madness was dispelled.

It had been less than a year earlier when a young footman,

frightened by Octave's face, had made as if to obstruct him as he was running out of his mother's drawing-room, and Octave in a fury had cried : "Who are you to set yourself up against me? If you're so strong, prove your strength!" And with these words he had seized the man bodily and flung him out of the window. The footman fell into the garden on top of an oleander in an urn, and was only slightly hurt. For two months Octave appointed himself the servant of the injured man; in the end he gave him too much money, and spent several hours every day furthering the fellow's education. As the whole family was anxious that he should keep silent, he received gifts and found himself overwhelmed with favours, so that he went to the bad and had to be sent back to his home in the country with a pension. In the light of this Mme de Malivert's anxieties are understandable.

What had frightened her most of all at the time of this depressing affair was that Octave, although he had repented utterly, had burst out with it only the next day. When he returned home that night, and was by chance reminded of the danger the man had incurred, he said : "He's young; why did he not defend himself? When he tried to stop me leaving, didn't I tell him to defend himself?" Mme de Malivert thought to have observed that these crises of fury possessed her son exactly at those moments when he seemed most forgetful of the sombre reverie which she habitually read in his expression. It had been, for instance, in the middle of a charade, after he had been cheerfully enjoying the company of several young men and half a dozen young ladies of his close acquaintance, that he had fled from the drawing-room and thrown the servant out of the window.

A few months before the evening of the two million francs, Octave had run away in much the same abrupt fashion from a ball given by Mme de Bonnivet. He had just danced several waltzes and quadrilles with remarkable grace. His mother was delighted at his success, and he himself must have been aware

29

of it; several women whose beauty had earned them great fame in society spoke to him in the most flattering way. His handsome fair hair, which fell in heavy curls across his superb forehead, had most of all impressed the celebrated Mme de Claix. And talking of fashion trends among young people in Naples, where she had recently been, she was paying him a very lively compliment, when suddenly Octave's face flushed red all over, and he left the drawing-room with a celerity which he tried in vain to disguise. His mother, in alarm, followed him but could not find him. She waited for him all night to no avail; he appeared only on the following day, and in a strange state; he had received three sabre-cuts, not very dangerous ones as it turned out. The doctors thought this monomania was a purely *moral* one— that was the word they used—and that it stemmed not from any physical cause, but from the influence of some strange idea. No symptoms heralded the migraines of M. le Vicomte Octave, as they used to be called. These crises had followed each other much more closely during his first year at the Ecole Polytechnique, before he had thought of becoming a priest. His comrades, with whom he frequently quarrelled, thought him completely mad on these occasions, and this notion often saved him from sword-thrusts.

While he was kept to his bed by the slight wounds of which we have just spoken, he had told his mother, as simply as was his wont: "I was furious, and picked a quarrel with some soldiers who were looking at me and laughing; I fought, and only got what I deserve;" after which he had talked of something else. With Armance de Zohiloff his cousin he had gone into greater detail. "I have moments of unhappiness and fury," he told her one evening, "which are not madness, although because of them I shall pass for a madman in society as I did at the Ecole Polytechnique. It's a misfortune like any other, but what outmatches my courage is the fear of finding that all of a sudden I have cause for eternal remorse, as nearly happened to me in the case of poor Pierre's accident."

"You've made amends nobly for that; you used to give him not only your allowance but your time as well, and if he had had any honest principles at all you would have made his fortune. What more could you do?"

"Nothing, certainly, once the accident had happened, or it would have been monstrous not to have done it. But that's not all; these crises of unhappiness which look to everyone like madness seem to set me apart from other people. I see that young men of my own age, apparently the poorest, the most limited, the most unfortunate of their kind, have one or two childhood friends who share their joys and their sorrows. In the evening I see them going for walks together, and telling each other all that interests them. I find that I alone am lonely on this earth. I have not and never shall have anyone to whom I can freely confide my thoughts. What then of my feelings, if I should have any tugging at my heart? Am I destined always to live without friends, and almost without acquaintances? Am I evil?" he concluded with a sigh.

"Certainly not," replied Armance with all the severity of friendship, trying to hide the too real pity she felt for his grief, "but you give occasion to those who do not like you. For instance, why didn't you turn up at the ball given by Mme de Claix the day before yesterday, you who are so perfectly polite to everybody?"

"Because it was her idiotic compliments at the ball six months ago which earned me the shame of being in the wrong with those young sabre-carrying peasants."

"Very well," answered Mlle de Zohiloff, "but notice that you always find excuses for not meeting society. So you mustn't go on to complain of the isolation in which you live."

"Ah, it's friends I need, not just meeting society. Am I likely to find a friend in those salons?"

"Yes, since you couldn't find one at the Ecole Polytechnique."

"You're right," replied Octave after a long silence; "at this moment I see things as you do, and tomorrow, when it comes to acting, I shall act in a way opposite to what seems reasonable to me today, and all because of pride! Oh, if heaven had ordained me to be the son of a cloth merchant I should have been working at a counter from the age of sixteen; instead of which every occupation I have had has been a luxury, no more; I would have had less pride and more happiness. . . . Oh, how I dislike what I am!"

These woes, although apparently egoistic, were interesting to Armance; Octave's eyes expressed so great a possibility of love, and sometimes they were so tender!

She felt, without being really clear about it, that Octave was the victim of that kind of irrational sensibility which makes men unhappy and worthy to be loved. A passionate imagination led him to overrate the forms of happiness in which he could not share. Had heaven endowed him with a dry, cold, reasoning heart, besides all the other assets he combined, he might have been very happy indeed. All he lacked was an average soul.

It was only in his cousin's company that Octave sometimes dared to think aloud. It will be clear why he had been so painfully affected by the discovery that the feelings of this charming cousin varied according to fortune.

The day after Octave had wished for death he was awakened abruptly, no later than seven in the morning, by his uncle the Commandeur, who came into his room affecting to make a shocking din. The man was never free from affectation. The anger roused in Octave by this noise lasted less than three seconds; the idea of duty then supervened, and he received M. de Soubirane in the light, pleasant manner which suited him best.

This spirit of common clay who, birth or no birth, saw nothing in the world but money, explained at great length to the noble Octave that one must not go quite out of one's mind with happiness when an annual income of twenty-five thousand francs turned into the hope of a hundred thousand. This philosophic and almost christian dissertation ended with advice to speculate on the Bourse as soon as one had gained possession of a twentieth of the two million. The Marquis would certainly place a part of this increased wealth at Octave's disposal; but no speculation should be undertaken except upon the advice of the Commandeur; he knew Mme la Comtesse de ∗∗∗, and dealing in stock could be a *complete certainty*. At the words *complete certainty* Octave drew himself up with a start. "Yes, my friend," said the Commandeur, who took the movement for a gesture of doubt, "a *complete certainty*. I have neglected the Comtesse a little since her ridiculous behaviour at M. le Prince de S ∗∗∗'s; but after all we are distantly related, and I'm leaving you now to go and find our mutual friend the Duc de ∗∗∗ who will reconcile us."

A 2

CHAPTER IV

Half a dupe, half duping, the first
deceived perhaps by her deceit and fair
words, as all those philosophers. Philosophers they say? mark this, Diego,
the devil can cite scripture for his
purpose. O, what a goodly outside
falsehood hath!

Massinger

THE COMMANDEUR'S absurd visit almost plunged Octave once more into his misanthropy of the previous day. His loathing for mankind was at its peak, when his servant brought him a large book, very carefully wrapped in English vellum paper. The impression of the seal was beautifully cut, but the subject unattractive: on a field sable a saltire of two bones. Octave, whose taste was impeccable, admired the accuracy with which the two tibias were drawn and the perfection of the engraving. "That's from the school of Pikler," he thought to himself; "it must be some wild idea of my devout cousin Mme de C ∗∗∗." He realized his mistake on finding a magnificent Bible, bound by Thouvenin. "The devout don't give Bibles," said Octave, opening the covering letter; but he sought the signature in vain, for there was none, and he threw the letter into the hearth. A moment later his servant, old Saint-Jacques, entered with a sly look.

"Who sent this parcel?" asked Octave.

"It's all a mystery, an attempt to avoid M. le Vicomte's

34

notice; but it's only old Perrin who left it at the porter's, and ran off like a thief."

"And what is old Perrin?"

"He is one of Mme la Marquise de Bonnivet's men, who to all appearance has been dismissed, and who is now sent on secret errands."

"Is Mme de Bonnivet suspected of having an affair of some sort?"

"Oh, good gracious, no, sir! The secret errands are for the new religion. It is perhaps a Bible, sir, that Mme la Marquise has secretly sent you. You will have been able to recognise the handwriting of Mme Rouvier, lady's-maid to Mme la Marquise."

Octave looked into the fireplace and ordered the letter to be given back to him, since it had fluttered beyond the flames and was not burnt at all. It was well known, he saw to his surprise, that he read Helvétius, Bentham, Bayle and other evil books. He was reproached for it. "The most spotless virtue is no guarantee against it:" he thought to himself; "no sooner does one become a sectarian than one stoops to intrigue and employs spies. Since the law of indemnity, it seems, I have become worthy to have an interest taken in my salvation and in the influence which I may one day wield."

Throughout the rest of the day the conversation of the Marquis de Malivert, the Commandeur and the two or three true friends who were sent for and invited to dinner, alluded almost continuously and with a notable lack of taste to Octave's marriage and to his new position. Still shaken by the moral crisis which he had had to undergo the night before, he was less icy than usual. His mother thought he looked paler, and he set himself the task, if not of being cheerful, at least of appearing to dwell solely upon ideas pleasantly associated; so cleverly did he go about it that he succeeded in deluding those who surrounded him. Nothing could stop him, not even the Commandeur's witticisms about the prodigious effect of two million

35

upon a philosopher's mind. Octave took advantage of his feigned heedlessness to say that even if he were a prince he would not marry until he was twenty-six—which was the age at which his father had married.

"Obviously that boy cherishes the secret ambition to become a bishop or a cardinal," said the Commandeur the moment Octave left the room; "his birth and his doctrine will earn him a red hat."

This remark, which drew a smile from Mme de Malivert, awoke lively anxiety in the Marquis. "Say what you like," he countered in answer to his wife's smile, "the only people with whom my son is on fairly intimate terms are churchmen and young scholars of the same persuasion, and—something that's never been known in my family—he shows a marked distaste for young fellows in the Army."

"There's something strange about the young man," pursued M. de Soubirane. This observation caused Mme de Malivert to sigh in her turn.

Octave, bored to distraction by having had to talk, had left early to go to the Gymnase; he could not abide the wit in M. Scribe's charming plays. "And yet," he told himself, "nothing has been more genuinely successful, and to despise without knowledge is so common an absurdity in my circle that I can earn no merit by staying away." He submitted himself in vain to the experiment throughout two of the prettiest sketches at the Théâtre de Madame. The pleasantest and subtlest words seemed to him tainted with coarseness, and the key which is given back in the second act of *Le Mariage de Raison* drove him out of the theatre. He entered a restaurant and, true to the mysteriousness of all his actions, ordered candles and some soup; when the soup was brought he locked himself in, read with interest two newspapers he had just bought, burned them in the fireplace with the greatest care, paid and walked out. He came home and dressed, and on that evening experienced a certain eagerness to appear at Mme de Bonnivet's. "Who could

36

say for certain," he wondered, "that that wicked Duchesse d'Ancre hasn't slandered Mlle de Zohiloff? After all, my uncle is convinced that my head has been turned by those two million." Octave was gladdened by this idea, which had occurred to him through some unimportant word he had read in one of his newspapers. His mind dwelt upon Armance, but as upon his only friend, or rather upon the only being who was almost a friend to him.

He was very far from any thought of loving; he held that sentiment in horror. His soul that day, strengthened by virtue and misfortune, and itself nought but virtue and strength, was simply afraid of having too lightly condemned *a friend*.

Octave never once looked at Armance; but his eyes did not miss a single one of her movements all through the evening. On entering the drawing-room he began by paying marked attention to the Duchesse d'Ancre; his conversation with her was so profoundly attentive that the good lady had the pleasure of believing him converted to a proper regard for her rank. "Since acquiring hopes of wealth, this philosopher is of our party," she murmured to Mme de la Ronze.

Octave wished to ascertain the degree of the woman's perversity; to discover her very wicked was somehow to find Mlle de Zohiloff innocent. He observed that the sentiment of hatred alone breathed a certain life into the shrivelled heart of Mme d'Ancre; but conversely, it was only generous and noble things which inspired her with aversion. It seemed as though she felt the need to avenge herself upon them. Ignobility and baseness of feeling, but ignobility couched in the most elegant terms, were alone privileged to bring a sparkle to the little eyes of the Duchesse.

Octave was considering how to extricate himself from the interest with which he was being listened to, when he heard Mme de Bonnivet asking for her chessboard. It was a little masterpiece of Chinese carving which M. l'Abbé Dubois had brought back from Canton. Octave seized the opportunity to escape from Mme d'Ancre, and begged his cousin to let him have the key of the cabinet in which this magnificent chess set was kept out of the way of the servants' clumsiness. Armance was no longer in the drawing-room; she had left a few moments earlier with her intimate friend Méry de Tersan; had Octave not requested the cabinet key, Mlle de Zohiloff's absence would have been unkindly noticed, and on her return she might have had to endure a quite restrained but very hard little glance of some kind. Armance was poor, and only eighteen, while Mme de Bonnivet was over thirty; she was still very beautiful, but Armance too was beautiful.

The two friends had stopped beside the fireplace of a large boudoir near the drawing-room. Armance had wanted to show Méry a portrait of Lord Byron, of which Mr. Philips, the English painter, had recently sent a print to her aunt. As he passed along the private corridor beside the boudoir, Octave heard these words very distinctly : "Ah, well! He's like all the rest! A soul I thought so fine, overwhelmed by the hope of two million!" The tones in which the highly flattering words '*I thought so fine*' were spoken left Octave thunderstruck; he stopped short. When he began to walk on, he stepped so lightly that not even the keenest ear could have heard him. As he returned past the boudoir with the chess set in his hand he paused for a moment, then blushed at his indiscretion and returned to the drawing-room. The remarks he had just overheard were not decisive in a world where envy can appear in every guise, but their tone of candour and honesty resounded in his heart. These were by no means the accents of envy.

When he had given the Marquise her Chinese chessmen, Octave felt the need for reflection; he moved over into a corner of the drawing-room behind a whist table, and there his imagination echoed twenty times over the sound of the words he had just heard. He had already been engaged for some time in this profound and delightful reverie, when his ear caught the sound of Armance's voice. He was not yet considering how best to regain his cousin's esteem; he was delighting in the happiness of having lost it. As he left the distant corner occupied by the peaceful whist-players, and drew near the group surrounding Mme de Bonnivet, Armance noticed the look in his eyes; they lighted on her with that kind of softening and weariness which, after great joy, seems to rob them of the power to move swiftly.

Octave was not to find happiness a second time that day; he was unable to speak a single word to Armance. "Nothing is more difficult than to justify myself," he thought, while he pretended to listen to the promptings of the Duchesse d'Ancre, who, as they went last from the drawing-room, insisted upon driving him home. It was a dry, cold night with a magnificent moon; Octave ordered his horse and went riding for a few miles along the new boulevard. As he returned home at about three in the morning, without knowing why or noticing the fact, he rode past the Bonnivets' house.

CHAPTER V

Her glossy hair was cluster'd o'er a brow
Bright with intelligence, and fair and smooth;
Her eyebrow's shape was like the aerial bow,
Her cheek all purple with the beam of youth,
Mounting, at times, to a transparent glow,
As if her veins ran lightning . . .

Don Juan, Canto 1

"How can I prove to Mlle de Zohiloff by deeds and not by vain words, that the pleasure of seeing my father's fortune quadrupled has not entirely turned my head?" For twenty-four hours the attempt to find an answer to this question was Octave's sole preoccupation. For the first time in his life his soul was carried away without his realising it.

For many years he had invariably remained aware of his feelings and had exercised them upon objects which he considered reasonable. It was, nevertheless, with all the impatience of a young man of twenty that he awaited the time when he was to meet Mlle de Zohiloff. He had not the slightest doubt as to the feasibility of speaking to a young woman whom he saw twice almost every day; his only quandary was the choice of words most suitable to convince her. "For, after all," he said to himself, "in twenty-four hours I can't find an action which would prove conclusively that I am above the pettiness of which her inmost heart accuses me, and I must be allowed to make my first protestation in words." Many forms of words indeed occurred to him successively; one he would consider too

40

emphatic, while with another he would be afraid of treating so grave an imputation too lightly. He had still not decided what he ought to say to Mlle de Zohiloff, when eleven struck, and he arrived among the first in the drawing-room of the Bonnivets' house. But to his exceeding surprise he noticed that Mlle de Zohiloff, who spoke to him several times during the evening, apparently as usual, nevertheless denied him every opportunity of speaking a single word intended for her ear alone! Octave was severely piqued, and the evening passed like a flash.

The following day he was equally unfortunate; and the next day, and the days that followed, brought him no nearer speaking to Armance. Each day he hoped to find occasion to speak the word so essential to his honour, and each day, though not a hint of affectation could be perceived in Mlle de Zohiloff's behaviour, he saw his hopes vanish. He was losing the friendship and esteem of the one person who seemed to him worthy of his own, and all because he was believed to entertain feelings directly opposite to his real ones. Fundamentally, it was true, nothing was more flattering, but at the same time nothing was more irritating. Octave was deeply preoccupied with what was happening to him; it took him several days to become accustomed to his new position. Without realizing it, he who had so much loved silence fell into the habit of talking a great deal whenever Mlle de Zohiloff was within earshot. He cared little, in fact, whether he appeared strange or incoherent. Whatever brilliant or important woman he happened to be addresssing, he was really speaking to no one but Mlle de Zohiloff, and for her alone.

This real misfortune distracted Octave from his black dejection, and he forgot his habit of always seeking to assess the quantity of happiness he was enjoying at any given moment. He was losing his only friend, he saw himself denied an esteem which he felt sure he deserved; but these misfortunes, however cruel they might be, did not extend so far as to inspire him with that deep loathing for life which he had formerly experienced.

"What man has not been reviled?" he asked himself. "The severity with which I am treated at the moment is a guarantee of the eagerness with which this wrong will be righted when the truth is known at last."

Octave could see an obstacle between himself and happiness, but he could see the happiness, or at least the end of his sorrow, a sorrow upon which his mind dwelt exclusively. His life took on a new purpose; he passionately wished to regain Armance's esteem, and this was no easy undertaking. The girl had an unusual character. Born just within the confines of the Russian Empire near the Caucasian border, at Sebastopol where her father had a command, Mlle de Zohiloff concealed beneath a perfectly gentle appearance a firm will, worthy of the harsh climate in which her childhood had been spent. Her mother, a close relative of Mme de Bonnivet and Mme de Malivert, while at Mittau with the court of Louis XVIII, had married a Russian colonel. This officer, M. de Zohiloff, belonged to one of the noblest families in the Moscow government; but his father and grandfather had had the misfortune to associate themselves with favourites who were shortly afterwards sent to Siberia, and so had seen their riches rapidly dwindle.

Armance's mother died in 1811; she lost her father General de Zohiloff shortly afterwards, killed at the battle of Montmirail. When Mme de Bonnivet heard that she had a relative all alone in a little town in farthest Russia, with no more than a hundred louis a year, she lost no time in arranging for her to come to France. She styled her a niece and hoped to marry her off, assisted by a measure of favour at court; Armance's maternal great-grandfather had been a Knight of the Order of the Holy Ghost. It will be evident that, even though barely eighteen, Mlle de Zohiloff had already known considerable misfortune. Perhaps that was why the trivialities of life seemed to slip past her without contriving to trouble her soul. Sometimes it was not impossible to read in her eyes that she could be deeply moved, but it was clear that no vulgarity could ever succeed in affecting her. This perfect serenity, which it would have been so flattering to make her forget for a moment, was combined, in her, with the subtlest intelligence, and earned her a respect beyond that due her years.

This unusual character, and above all her large dark blue eyes with their bewitching glances, won her the friendship of all women of refinement in Mme de Bonnivet's circle; but Mlle de Zohiloff also had many enemies. Her aunt had sought in vain to correct her complete inability to pay the slightest attention to people she did not like. It was only too clear that while she was speaking to them her mind was elsewhere. There were besides a number of little quirks of speech and behaviour which Armance would not have dared to condemn in other women; perhaps it never even occurred to her to shun them herself; but had she allowed herself to use them, she would have blushed for many a long day whenever she recalled them. From her earliest years her feelings about childish trifles had been so violent that she had strongly reproached herself for them. She had fallen into the habit of judging herself hardly at all in terms of the effect produced on others, but a great deal in terms of her feelings at any given time, the recollection of which was apt to poison her life the day after.

One perceived something asiatic in the girl's features, and also in her gentleness and unconcern, which, despite her age, still seemed childlike. None of her actions directly suggested the idea of the exaggerated feeling about what a woman owes to herself, and yet a certain enchantingly restrained and gracious charm surrounded her. Without in any way seeking to attract notice, and at every turn ignoring opportunities to score a success, the girl aroused interest. It was evident that Armance did not permit herself a host of things which are sanctioned by custom and which are daily to be observed in the behaviour of the most refined women. In short I have no doubt that, but for her extreme gentleness and youth, Mlle de Zohiloff's enemies would have accused her of prudishness.

43

Her foreign upbringing and her late coming to France still served to extenuate what the eye of hatred might have marked as slightly strange in her reactions to events, and even in her behaviour.

Octave spent his life among people whose enmity had been aroused by this unusual character of Mlle de Zohiloff's; the high favour in which she stood with Mme de Bonnivet was a source of grievance unforgivable to the friends of that woman so greatly respected in society. Her impassive uprightness frightened them. As it is rather difficult to impugn a girl's behaviour, her beauty was attacked instead. Octave was the first to agree that his young cousin might easily have been much prettier. She was remarkable by what, if I dared, I should call her Russian beauty; it was a combination of features which, while it expressed very strongly a simplicity and devotion no longer to be found among over-civilized peoples, conveyed, it must be admitted, a strange mixture of the purest Circassian beauty and certain German characteristics a little too early in prominence. There was nothing common in the contour of those features, which were so deeply serious, but a little too expressive, even at rest, to correspond exactly to the idea prevalent in France of what a girl's beauty ought properly to be.

To those accused before the generous-minded, it is of great advantage if their faults are first recited by enemy tongues. When the hatred of Mme de Bonnivet's good friends condescended so low as to be openly jealous of Armance's meagre little existence, they made a great many jokes about the unpleasant effect of too prominent a brow and features which, seen from the front, were perhaps a little too pronounced.

The only way in which Armance's expression really laid itself open to her enemies was by the presence of a strange look in her eyes now and then, when she least realized it. This deep, fixed look was one of extreme concentration; certainly it held nothing which could shock the strictest delicacy; there was neither coquetry nor assurance to be seen in it; but there was no denying it was strange, and on that score unbecoming to a young woman. Mme de Bonnivet's sycophants, when they were sure she was looking at them, sometimes mimicked this look as they spoke of Armance among themselves; but in their vulgarity they robbed it of that which they could never perceive in it. "In just such a way," Mme de Malivert told them one day, out of all patience with their unkindness, "would two angels, exiled among mankind, and compelled to hide themselves in mortal guise, look at each other for recognition."

It will be agreed that it was no easy matter, by adroit hints, to clear oneself of a grave injustice, in the eyes of someone so firm in her beliefs, and of so straightforward a character. To succeed in doing so Octave would have required a presence of mind and, more important, a degree of assurance, beyond his years.

If Armance, without intending it, showed him by a word that she no longer regarded him as an intimate friend, his heart would sink, and he would be struck dumb for a quarter of an hour. He was far from discovering, in Armance's way of expressing herself, any pretext upon which to refute her and regain his rights. Sometimes he tried to speak, but he was too late, and his reply lacked apropos; and yet it carried a certain air of earnestness. In his vain search for ways to clear himself of the accusation covertly levelled at him by Armance, Octave unwittingly let it be seen how deeply he was affected by it; it was perhaps the cleverest way of earning his pardon.

Ever since the decision taken upon the law of indemnity had become common knowledge, even among the mass of society, Octave, to his great surprise, found himself a person of some distinction. He discovered that important people were taking an interest in him. He was treated in an entirely new way, especially by very great ladies who could regard him as a potential husband for their daughters. This mania of the mothers in this century to be for ever husband-hunting shocked Octave almost beyond words. The Duchesse de ∗∗∗, to whom he had the honour to be slightly related, and who had seldom if ever spoken to him before the law was passed, judged it necessary to apologise for not having kept him a seat in the box she had reserved at the Gymnase Theatre for the following day. "My dear cousin," she said to him, "I am aware of all your prejudice against that pretty kind of play—the only kind I enjoy." "I admit I am wrong," replied Octave, "and the authors are in the right, and their pointed remarks are in no way tainted with coarseness; but this recantation is not leading up to a request for a seat. I confess that I am ill-adapted either for society or for this type of comedy which is apparently a pleasant facsimile of it." This misanthropic tone in so handsome a young man struck the Duchesse's two little daughters as thoroughly ridiculous, and they joked about it all the evening, but none the less the following day their behaviour towards Octave showed *perfect simplicity*. He noticed the change and shrugged his shoulders.

Surprised at his own popularity, and even more at how little effort it was costing him, Octave, being accomplished in the theory of life, expected to suffer the attacks of envy; "because," he told himself, "this indemnity must certainly procure me that pleasure too." He did not have to wait very long for it; only a few days later he was informed that certain young officers in Mme de Bonnivet's circle were full of ready jests about his new fortune. "What a shame for poor Malivert," one of them would say; "those two million dropping on his head like a ton of bricks! He'll never be able to become a priest now. It's very hard luck!" "One simply can't conceive," another would continue, "how in this century, when the nobility is so rudely beset, a man can dare to sport a title and evade the baptism of blood." "Yet it's the only virtue which the Jacobins have not so far thought of condemning as hypocrisy," a third would add.

Following upon these remarks, Octave went out more, appeared at every ball, was exceedingly haughty, and even, so far as his nature allowed, was rude to the young men; but all to no

46

avail. To his great surprise (he was only twenty), he found that he was respected the more for it. As a matter of fact it was decided that the indemnity had quite turned his head, but most women went on to add : "That free, proud look was the only thing he lacked!" That was the name they insisted on giving to what he himself thought of as insolence, something he would never have allowed himself to display had he not been told of the unpleasant remarks made about him. Octave enjoyed the surprisingly warm welcome given him in society, a welcome so well matched with his natural disposition to stand aloof. His popularity pleased him chiefly because of the happiness he read in his mother's eyes; it was at the repeated instance of Mme de Malivert that he had forsaken his cherished solitude. But the most general effect of the attentions of which he found himself the centre was to remind him of the disfavour of Mlle de Zohiloff. It seemed to increase day by day. There were moments when this disfavour amounted almost to a want of politeness; it was at best a most markedly distant manner, and the more noticeable in that the new existence which Octave owed to the indemnity was nowhere more manifest than in the Bonnivets' house.

Now that he might one day find himself the leader of an influential salon, the Marquise wished at all costs to wrest him from that arid philosophy of the *useful*. For several months she had been using this name to describe what is generally called eighteenth-century philosophy. "When are you going to throw those books into the fire?" she would ask him; "the authors are such dismal men, and you alone, of the young people of your age and rank, continue to read them."

It was to a kind of German mysticism that Mme de Bonnivet hoped to convert Octave. She condescended to investigate with him whether he possessed a *sense of religion*. Octave classed this attempt at conversion among the strangest things that had befallen him since he had abandoned the solitary life. "Here's one of those acts of madness," he thought, "which one

47

could never foresee."

Mme la Marquise de Bonnivet might have been described as one of the most prominent women in society. Perfectly regular features, very large eyes with the most commanding aspect, a superb figure and a very noble manner—a little too noble, perhaps—placed her in the forefront wherever she went. Rather large drawing-rooms made an extremely good setting for Mme de Bonnivet, and on the opening day of the last session of the chambers, for example, her name had been mentioned first among the most brilliant women. Octave foresaw with pleasure the effect that would be produced by the research *into the sense of religion*. This being who thought himself so free of falsehood could not avoid a stirring of pleasure at the idea of the false interpretation which the public were going to infer on his account.

The exalted virtue of Mme de Bonnivet was above the reach of calumny. Her imagination was entirely concerned with God and angels, or at the very most with certain beings intermediary between God and man, who—according to the most modern German philosophers—hover about a few feet above our heads. It is from this elevated though adjacent position that they *magnetize our souls*, etc., etc. Octave reflected that Mme de Bonnivet was going to risk for his sake that reputation for wisdom which she had so justly enjoyed ever since she entered society, and which the scholarly hints of the secular jesuits had been unable to discredit; and the pleasure of unmistakably attracting the attention of so eminent a woman led him to bear patiently the long explanations she considered necessary to convert him.

Among his new acquaintances Octave was soon regarded as the inseparable friend of this Marquise de Bonnivet, who was so celebrated in certain circles, and who, as she herself saw it, created a sensation at court when she condescended to appear there. Although the Marquise was a very great and fashionable lady and was, besides, still very beautiful, these advantages made no impression at all on Octave; he had the misfortune to discern something a little affected in her behaviour, and no sooner did he perceive this fault anywhere than he felt disinclined to be anything but derisive. But this sage of twenty was far from fathoming the real cause of his pleasure in allowing himself to be converted. He who had so often sworn himself solemn oaths against love that it could be said that hatred of the passion was the chief concern of his life, now went with pleasure to the Bonnivets' house because that same Armance who despised him—hated him perhaps—was always within a few steps of her aunt. Octave was in no way presumptuous; the worst failing of his character was even to overestimate his disadvantages, but if he had any self-esteem at all it was concerned with honour and strength of mind. He had dissociated himself without the slightest ostentation or weakness from several opinions, ridiculous ones but pleasant to share, which stand as principles for most young people of his class and age.

These victories which he could not conceal from himself, for example his love of soldiering, quite untinged with any ambition for rank or promotion, these victories, I say, had inspired him with great confidence in his own resolution. "It's cowardice and not lack of lights that stops us reading our own hearts," he used to say occasionally, and supported by this fine principle he relied a little too much on his insight. A single word revealing to him that he might one day feel love for Mlle de Zohiloff would have caused him to leave Paris instantly; but as he stood then he was far removed from this idea. He held Armance in high and, so to speak, unique esteem; he saw himself despised by her and esteemed her precisely because she despised him. Was it not perfectly natural to wish to regain her esteem? There was no suspect desire to please the young woman in that. What was sufficient to remove even the slightest stirring of a suspicion that he might be in love was that when Octave found himself among Mlle de Zohiloff's enemies he was the first to admit her faults. But the state of anxiety and constantly dis-

49

appointed hope in which he was kept by his cousin's continued silence towards him prevented him from seeing that there was not a single one of those faults of which she was accused in his presence that did not, in his mind, have some kindred quality of greatness.

One day, for example, they were attacking Armance's preference for short hair falling in great big curls around the head, such as they wear in Moscow. "Mlle de Zohiloff finds that style convenient," said one of the Marquise's sycophants; "she doesn't like to spend too much time at her toilette." Octave's maliciousness noticed pleasurably the success which this remark achieved among the women of the circle. They let it be understood that Armance was right to sacrifice everything to the duties imposed on her by her affection for her aunt, and, their looks seemed to say, to sacrifice everything to her duties as a lady companion. Octave's pride was far from the thought of replying to this insinuation. While maliciousness enjoyed it, he indulged silently in the delight of a little stirring of passionate admiration. He felt rather than formulated : "this woman attacked thus by all the others is nevertheless the only one here worthy of my esteem! She is as poor as the other women are rich, and she alone might be forgiven for exaggerating the importance of money. And yet she despises it, she who hasn't a thousand écus a year; and it is uniquely and basely adored by these women who all of them enjoy the greatest affluence."

CHAPTER VI

Cromwell, I charge thee, fling away ambition;
By that sin fell the angels, how can man then,
The image of his Maker, hope to win by't?
King Henry VIII, Act III

O NE EVENING, when the card players had been settled, and the great ladies whom Mme de Bonnivet took the trouble to greet had arrived, she was in singularly interested conversation with Octave : "Your whole being is quite beyond my conception," she was telling him for the hundredth time.

"If you were to swear to me," he replied, "that you would never betray my secret, I would confide it to you; and no one has ever known it before."

"What, not even Mme de Malivert?"

"My respect forbids me to trouble her."

Mme de Bonnivet, despite the high ideals of her belief, was not by any means immune from the charm of knowing the great secret of one of the men who, in her eyes, approached most nearly to perfection; besides, the secret had never been told before.

Upon Octave's enjoining eternal discretion Mme de Bonnivet left the drawing-room and returned a few moments later with a curious ornament dangling from her gold watch-chain; it was a kind of iron cross manufactured in Kœnigsberg; she took it in her left hand and said to Octave in a low, solemn voice : "You ask me for eternal secrecy, in every circumstance,

51

from every person. I *vow by Jehovah*, yea, I will keep that secret."

"Well, Madame," said Octave, amused by this little ceremony and the ritualistic manner of his noble cousin, "the thing that often fills my soul with darkness, that I have never disclosed to anyone, is this horrible misfortune: I have no *conscience* at all. I find within myself none of what you call the *inmost sense,* no *instinctive* aversion from crime. Even if I abhor vice, it is quite vulgarly as a result of reasoning, and because I consider it harmful. And what proves to me that there is nothing divine or *instinctive* in me is that I can always recall every step in the reasoning by virtue of which vice horrifies me."

"Ah, how I pity you, my dear cousin; my heart grieves for you!" said Mme de Bonnivet in a tone which betrayed the liveliest pleasure; "you are precisely what we call the *rebel being."*

At that moment her interest in Octave was plainly visible to certain shrewd observers—for they were under observation. Her gestures lost all affectation and assumed a certain solemnity and genuineness; her eyes darted a gentle ardour as she listened to this handsome young man, and especially as she expressed her pity for him. Mme de Bonnivet's good friends, who were watching her from a distance, hastened to draw the boldest conclusions, whereas in fact she was transported merely by the pleasure of having at last found a *rebel being*. Octave promised fair to be a memorable victory for her if she succeeded in awakening *conscience* and the *inmost sense* in him. A famous physician of the last century, summoned to a friend of his, a great nobleman, silently examined the symptoms of the disease for some time, then suddenly cried out in a transport of joy: "Ah, M. le Marquis, this is an illness that has been lost since ancient times! *Vitreous catarrh!* A superb disease, absolutely fatal. Oh, I've found it again, I've found it again!" Mme de Bonnivet's joy was of this order; in a way it was an artist's joy.

52

Ever since she had devoted herself to spreading the New Protestantism, which is to succeed Christianity whose day is done, and which, as we know, is on the point of going through its Fourth Metamorphosis, she had heard talk of *rebel beings*; they constitute the sole objection to the system of German mysticism based upon the existence of the inner conscience of good and evil. She was fortunate enough to have discovered one of them; she alone of all the world knew his secret, and this *rebel being* was perfect, because, as his moral conduct happened to be strictly honourable, no suspicion of personal interest crept in to mar the purity of his *diabolicism*.

I shall certainly not relate all the good reasons given that day by Mme de Bonnivet to persuade Octave that he did possess an *inmost sense*. The reader may perhaps not have had the good fortune to find himself within two or three paces of a charming cousin who despises him with all her heart, and whose friendship he burns to recapture. "This inmost sense, as its name implies, cannot manifest itself by any exterior sign; but nothing is simpler or easier to understand," said Mme de Bonnivet, "you are a *rebel being*, etc., etc. Do you not see, do you not feel, that beyond space and time there is nothing real here on earth . . . ?"

Throughout all this fine disquisition there shone in the eye of the Vicomte de Malivert a joy which was genuinely a little diabolical, and Mme de Bonnivet, who was in other respects a woman of great penetration, cried : "Ah, my dear Octave, *rebellion* shows plainly in your eyes !" It must be admitted that those large dark eyes, usually so discouraged, whose brilliance flashed under the most handsome fair curly hair in all the world, were at that moment extremely moving. They possessed that charm perhaps better understood in France than anywhere else : they revealed a soul, believed for many years to be of ice, which suddenly comes to life for you. The electrifying effect produced upon Mme de Bonnivet by that instant of perfect beauty and the fervent simplicity he conveyed in his

53

tones made her look really entrancing. In that instant she would have gone to martyrdom to ensure the triumph of her new religion; generosity and devotion blazed in her eyes. What a triumph for the maliciousness that watched her!

And these two beings, the most striking pair in the drawing-room where all unwittingly they were placing themselves on show, had no thought of attracting each other; indeed nothing was further from their minds. This was something which would have seemed utterly incredible to Mme la Duchesse d'Ancre and her neighbours, the sharpest ladies in all France. That is how matters of sentiment are judged in society.

Armance had been perfectly consistent in the position she had adopted against her cousin. Several months had elapsed since she had ceased to speak to him of their personal, private concerns. Often she would not say a word to him the whole evening, and Octave was beginning to take note of the days when she had condescended to be aware of his presence.

As he was careful not to appear put out by Mlle de Zohiloff's hatred, Octave was no longer noticeable in society by his invincible silence and the strange yet perfect nobility of expression with which his beautiful eyes had hitherto seemed to endure the tedium. He talked a great deal, entirely heedless of the absurdities into which he might be carried away. He thus became without knowing it one of the most fashionable men in those salons which, so to speak, hinged upon Mme de Bonnivet's. His perfect indifference to everything gave him a real superiority over his rivals; he came quite without pretensions among people who were eaten up with them. His *renown*, shining down from the illustrious Marquise de Bonnivet's salon into the circles where she was envied, had placed him, without any effort on his part, in a very pleasant position. Without as yet having done anything, he found that from his very first début in society he was classed as a being apart. Even the disdainful silence which suddenly came over him in the presence of people whom he thought incapable of understanding lofty feelings passed for piquant originality. Mlle de Zohiloff noted this popularity and was surprised by it. For the last three months Octave had been a different man. It was no wonder that his conversation, which everyone considered so brilliant, held a secret charm for Armance; its only aim was to please her.

Towards the middle of winter, Armance thought that Octave was about to make a very grand match, and it was easy to assess the social position to which the young Vicomte de Malivert had taken only a few months in rising. Occasionally in Mme de Bonnivet's drawing-room there was to be seen a very great nobleman, who had spent all his life on the look-out for things or people who were going to be in fashion. His hobby was to attach himself to them, and this singular urge had gained him considerable success; although a rank commoner, he had lifted himself to distinction. This great lord, as servile towards ministers as a shopboy, was on the best of terms with them, and he had a grand-daughter, his only heiress, for whose husband he could secure the greatest honours and advantages at the disposal of a monarchical government. All through the winter he had seemed to notice Octave, but no one had foreseen to what heights the young Vicomte's favour would rise. M. le Duc d *** was holding a large stag-hunting party in his forests in Normandy. It was a rare privilege to be his guest; and for thirty years he had not sent out a single invitation whose motives could not be guessed by the shrewd.

Suddenly, and without forewarning, he wrote a charming note to the Vicomte de Malivert and invited him to come hunting.

It was decided by Octave's family, who were all perfectly informed about the ways and character of the old Duc de ***, that if he were a success during his visit to the Château de Ranville, they would live to see him a duke and a peer. He departed laden with good advice from the Commandeur and the rest of the household; he had the honour to see a stag and four fine dogs hurl themselves into the Seine from a rock a hundred feet high, and on the third day he was back in Paris.

"Apparently you're quite mad," Mme de Bonnivet told him in the presence of Armance. "Is the young lady not to your liking?" "I have hardly inspécted her," he replied very coolly, "she even seems very pleasant; but when the hour of my visit here came round, I felt a gloom darken my soul."

After this grand stroke of philosophy the religious discussions were resumed more hotly than ever. To Mme de Bonnivet Octave seemed an astonishing being. At last an instinct for the proprieties, if I may hazard the expression, or the detection of an occasional smile, led the beautiful Marquise to understand that a drawing-room where a hundred people meet every night is not exactly the best place in the world to select for *the investigation of rebellion*. One day she asked Octave to call on her the following noon, after the midday meal. These were the words Octave had waited a long time to hear.

The next day was one of the finest in April. A delightful breeze and wafts of warmth heralded the coming of spring. It occurred to Mme de Bonnivet to remove her theological conference into the garden. She anticipated that she could draw from the *ever-renewed* spectacle of Nature some striking argument in support of one of the fundamental tenets of her philosophy : *Whatever is very Beautiful is, of necessity, always True*. The Marquise did indeed speak extremely well, and at some length, until called away by a lady's-maid for a social duty owed to a foreign princess. The engagement had been fixed a week before, but her interest in the new religion, of which Octave was one day to be the St. Paul, had driven all else from her head. As the Marquise felt herself to be in excellent form, she begged Octave to await her return, and added : "Armance will keep you company."

The moment Mme de Bonnivet was out of earshot, Octave went on without the slightest timidity, for timidity is the daughter of love that knows itself and aspires : "Do you know, cousin, what my *conscience* tells me? That for the last three months you have despised me for a vulgar fellow whose head has been completely turned by the hope of increased wealth. I have long sought to justify myself to you, not by vain words but by deeds. I can find none which is conclusive, and I too have no recourse except to appeal to your *inmost sense*. Now this is what has happened to me. While I am speaking, watch my eyes to see whether I lie." And Octave proceeded to relate to his young cousin, in full detail and perfect simplicity, the whole sequence of feelings and actions with which we have acquainted the reader. He was careful not to forget the remark Armance had made to her friend Méry de Tersan, which he had overheard as he went to fetch the Chinese chessmen. "That remark has ordered my life; from that moment I have thought of nothing but regaining your esteem." Armance was deeply moved by this recollection, and a few silent tears began to trickle down her cheeks.

She did not interrupt Octave at all, and when he had finished she remained silent for a long time. "You believe me guilty!" Octave said, greatly affected by her silence. She did not reply. "I have lost your esteem," he cried, with a quiver of tears in his eyes. "Show me but one action in all the world by which I can regain the place I formerly held in your heart, and it shall be done on the instant." These last words, spoken with a deep, restrained energy, were too much for Armance's courage; it was no longer possible to pretend; tears welled into her eyes, and she wept openly. She feared that Octave might add some word that would increase her agitation and cause her to lose the last shred of self-control she still possessed. Most of all she was afraid to speak. In haste she held out her hand to him, and making a great effort to speak, and speak only as a friend, she said: "You have all my esteem." She was very relieved to see a maid approaching in the distance; the necessity of hiding her tears from this girl gave her a pretext for leaving the garden.

CHAPTER VII

But passion most dissembles yet betrays
Even by its darkness; as the blackest sky
Foretells the heaviest tempest, it displays
Its workings through the vainly guarded eye,
And in whatever aspect it arrays
Itself, 'tis still the same hypocrisy;
Coldness or anger, even disdain or hate,
Are masks it often wears, and still too late.

Don Juan, Canto I

OCTAVE REMAINED motionless, his eyes filled with tears, not knowing whether to rejoice or grieve. After waiting so long he had at last, then, been able to wage that battle he had so much wished for, but had he won or lost? "If I've lost it," he thought, "it will be the end of everything for me. Armance thinks me so guilty that she pretends to accept the first excuse I offer, and does not condescend to enter into explanations with a man so little deserving of her friendship. What do they mean, those brief words: *You have all my esteem*? Could anything be colder than that? Is this a perfect return to the old intimacy? Is that a polite way of cutting short disagreeable explanations?" Armance's leaving him so abruptly seemed to him a particularly bad omen.

While Octave, a prey to profound astonishment, strove to remember exactly what had just happened to him, tried to draw conclusions from it, and trembled, in the midst of his efforts to reason clearly, lest he should suddenly reach some decisive discovery which would put an end to uncertainty by proving that his cousin found him unworthy of her esteem, Armance was beset by the keenest sorrow. Her tears choked her, but they were tears of shame, and no longer of joy.

She hastened to lock herself into her room. "Great Heavens," she thought in her extreme confusion, "what ever will Octave think of the state he saw me in? Did he understand my tears? Alas, how can I doubt it? Since when has a simple confidence between friends called forth sobs from a girl my age? Oh, Lord, after shaming myself in this way how can I dare appear before him again? All that was lacking to complete the horror of my position was that I should deserve his contempt. But," said Armance to herself, "it was not such a simple confidence after all; for three months I have avoided speaking to him; it's been a sort of reconciliation between friends who had quarrelled, and they say one weeps at that sort of reconciliation—yes, but one doesn't run away; one isn't thrown into the most violent agitation.

"Instead of being locked in my room in a flood of tears I ought to be in the garden, to go on talking to him, happy in the simple good fortune of friendship. Yes," said Armance, "I must return to the garden; perhaps Mme de Bonnivet isn't back yet." She rose and looked at herself in a mirror, to find that she was in no condition to appear before Octave. "Ah!" she exclaimed, sinking despairingly on to a chair, "I'm a wretched creature whose honour is ruined—and ruined in whose eyes? Octave's." Her sobs and her despair prevented her from thinking.

"And half an hour ago I was so contented, so happy even," she told herself bitterly a few moments later, "despite my fatal secret, and now I'm ruined, ruined for ever, beyond all remedy! Such an intelligent man will have perceived the whole extent of my weakness, a weakness of the kind which more than any other must shock the severity of his reason." Armance's tears choked her. Her state of violent agitation lasted for several hours, and induced a slight feverishness which earned her permission to remain in her room the whole evening.

The fever rose, and soon an idea took shape : "I am only half despicable, because, after all, I did not in so many words confess my fatal love. But judging by what has just happened I cannot answer for anything. An eternal barrier will have to be raised between Octave and myself. I shall have to take the veil; I'll choose whichever order allows the most solitude, some convent lying among high mountains, with a picturesque view. There I shall never hear mention of him." That idea is *duty,* the unhappy Armance told herself. From that moment the sacrifice was made. She did not express to herself, she sensed (to express it in detail would have been tantamount to doubting it), she sensed this truth : "from the moment I have perceived the path of *duty,* to fail to follow it instantly, blindly and unquestioningly, is to act like a vulgar soul; it's to be unworthy of Octave. How often he has told me that here is the secret sign by which one can recognize souls of nobility! Oh, I'll submit to your judgment, my dear, noble friend, Octave!" The fever emboldened her to speak this name in a low voice, and she found some happiness in repeating it.

Soon Armance saw herself as a nun. There were moments when she felt surprised at the worldly ornaments which decorated her little room. "That beautiful engraving of the Sistine Madonna which Mme de Malivert gave me; now I in my turn shall have to give it away," she thought; "it was chosen by Octave, who preferred it to the *Marriage of the Madonna.* Raphael's first picture. Even in those days, I remember, I was already arguing with him whether his choice was right, solely for the pleasure of seeing him defend it. Was I then in love with him without knowing it? Have I always loved him? Oh, I must tear this dreadful passion out of my heart." And the unhappy Armance, as she sought to forget her cousin, found his memory woven into all her past actions, even the most unimportant ones. She was alone, having dismissed her maid in order to be able to weep without constraint. She rang, and had her engravings taken into the next room. Soon the little bedroom was stripped bare and adorned only by its pretty, bright blue wallpaper. Was a nun allowed, she wondered, to have wallpaper in her cell? She thought this difficulty over for some time; her soul felt a need to determine exactly to what state she would be reduced in her cell; uncertainty about that was worse than all her ills, for it was her imagination which conjured them up. "No," she said to herself at last, "wallpaper can't be allowed; it wasn't invented in the days of the foundresses of religious orders; these orders originated in Italy, and Prince Tuboskin was telling us that the only decoration in so many fine monasteries was to have their walls whitewashed every year. Ah!" she pursued incoherently, "perhaps I ought to go and take the veil in Italy; my excuse would be my health.

"Oh, no! At least let me not leave Octave's native soil, at least let me continue to hear his language spoken." At that moment Méry de Tersan entered her room; the naked walls were a shock to the girl, and she turned pale as she approached her friend. Armance, overwrought by her fever and by a certain virtuous zeal which was yet another way of loving Octave, wished to bind herself by a disclosure. "I want to become a nun," she said to Méry. "What! Can the cold-heartedness of a certain person have gone so far as to wound your susceptibilities?" "Oh, heavens, no; I have nothing with which to reproach Mme de Bonnivet; she is as friendly towards me as she can be to a poor girl who is a nobody in society. She even feels some love for me when she's sorrowful, and she couldn't be kinder to anyone than she is to me. I should be unfair, my soul would befit my lowliness, if I were to reproach her at all." One of the last words in this reply brought tears to the eyes of Méry, who was rich, and had the noble feelings for which her illustrious family is distinguished. Without addressing each other except by their tears and their pressings of hands, the two friends spent a great part of the evening together.

Eventually Armance told Méry all her reasons for retiring into a convent, with one exception : what was to become of a poor girl in society, one who after all could not be married off to a small tradesman at the corner of the street? What fate could she expect? In a convent one depends only upon the Rule. If it be lacking in the entertainments provided by the fine arts or society wit, distractions in which she could indulge at Mme de Bonnivet's, at least there is no absolute necessity there to please anyone at all, nor humiliation if one does not succeed. Armance would have died of shame sooner than pronounce Octave's name. "It is the measure of my misfortune," she thought as she wept and clung to Méry, "that I cannot even ask the advice of the most devoted, the most virtuous friend."

While Armance was weeping in her room, Octave, acting on an impulse which despite his philosophy he was far from being able to explain, since he knew that he would not see Mlle de Zohiloff at all that evening, drew closer to the women whom ordinarily he neglected in favour of Mme de Bonnivet's religious arguments. It was already several months since Octave had begun to find himself plagued by advances which were the more annoying for being exceedingly polite. He had become misanthropic and touchy; as touchy as Alceste on the subject of marriageable daughters. The minute he heard any mention of a society woman with whom he was not acquainted, his first words were: "Has she a marriageable daughter?" More recently his prudence had even become chary of accepting a first reply in the negative. "Madame So-and-so may not have a marriageable daughter," he would say, "but might she not have a niece somewhere?"

While Armance was in a kind of delirium, Octave in search of distraction from the uncertainty into which the events of the morning had plunged him, not only spoke to all the women with nieces, but even engaged in conversation some of those redoubtable women with as many as three daughters. Perhaps such courageousness was made easier by the sight of the little chair where Armance usually sat next to Mme de Bonnivet's armchair; it had just been taken by one of the de Claix girls, whose fine German shoulders, set off to advantage by the lowness of Armance's little chair, were improving the occasion by displaying all their freshness. "What a difference!" Octave thought, or rather felt; "How humiliated my cousin would be by that which is Mlle de Claix's triumph! For her it's no more than permissible coquetry; she isn't even at fault; here again one could say: *Noblesse oblige.*" Octave began to flirt with Mlle de Claix. It would have required a certain interest to divine him, or more familiarity with his habitual simplicity of expression to recognize all the bitterness and contempt in the gaiety he affected. People were kind enough to find wit in what he said; the most applauded of his remarks seemed in his own view thoroughly commonplace and sometimes even tainted with coarseness. Since he had not stopped to talk to her at all that evening, Mme de Bonnivet chid him in an undertone as she passed close to him, and Octave justified his desertion in words that the Marquise found charming. She was very pleased with the wit of her proselyte-to-be, and with the social aplomb he was acquiring.

She sounded his praises with all the heartiness of innocence, if that word *heartiness* did not blush to be applied to a woman who took up such beautiful attitudes in her easy chair, and glanced towards heaven with such picturesque movements of the eyes. It must be confessed that occasionally, as she gazed fixedly at a gold moulding on her drawing-room ceiling, she reached the point of saying to herself : "There, in that empty space, there in the air, is a genius listening to me, magnetizing my soul and giving it those strange feelings which I really find quite unexpected, and which I sometimes express so eloquently." That evening Mme de Bonnivet, very pleased with Octave and with the position to which her disciple could one day attain, said to Mme de Claix : "All the young Vicomte really lacked was the assurance which wealth provides. Even if I didn't like that excellent law of indemnity for being so fair to our poor emigrés, I should like it for the new spirit it gives my cousin." Mme d'Ancre looked at Mme de Claix and Mme la Comtesse de la Ronze; and as Mme de Bonnivet left the ladies to go and receive a young duchess who was just arriving, Mme d'Ancre said to Mme de Claix: "All this seems to me abundantly clear."

"Only too clear," was the reply; "we are on the threshold of a scandal; a trifle more amiability from the *astonishing* Octave, and our dear Marquise will be unable to restrain herself from taking us entirely into her confidence."

"This is always the way they end, in my experience," rejoined Mme d'Ancre, "these great virtues that presume to dogmatize about religion. Ah, my fine Marquise, happy the woman who simply listens to her parish priest and takes her turn at providing his blessed bread!"

"That is certainly better than having Bibles bound by Thouvenin," added Mme de Claix.

But all Octave's assumed amiability had vanished in the twinkling of an eye. He had just seen Méry, who was on her way from Armance's room because her mother had called for her carriage—and Méry looked very much upset. She left so quickly that Octave was unable to speak to her. He himself went out at once. From that moment on he would have found it quite impossible to say a single word to anyone. Mlle de Tersan's expression of suffering told him that something extraordinary was happening; perhaps Mlle de Zohiloff was about to leave Paris to escape him. The admirable thing was that our philosopher had not the least idea that what he felt for Armance was love. He had made himself the strongest vows against that passion, and as penetration, not character, was what he lacked, he would probably have kept his word.

CHAPTER VIII

What shall I do the while? Where bide? How live?
Or in my life what comfort, when I am
Dead to him?   *Cymbeline, Act III*

ARMANCE WAS far from practising a similar self-deception. For a long time now seeing Octave had been her
one interest in life. When an unforeseen chance happened to change her young relative's social position, what
conflicts had rent her soul! What excuses had she not invented
to explain the sudden change wrought in Octave's behaviour!
And she was for ever asking herself: "Has he only a common
soul?"

By the time she reached the point of proving to herself that
Octave was made to feel happiness other than that which
comes from money and vanity, a new reason for sorrow had
intruded itself upon her. "I should be doubly scorned," she told
herself, "if my feeling for him were to be suspected; I, the
poorest girl that ever set foot in Mme de Bonnivet's drawing-
room. This profound unhappiness which threatened her on all
sides, and which ought to have spurred Armance to cure herself of her passion, in fact did no more, in plunging her into the
depths of melancholy, than thrust her more blindly towards the
one pleasure which remained to her, that of thinking about
Octave.

She saw him every day for several hours, and every day
trivial little events would occur to alter her way of thinking

about her cousin; how could she possibly have cured herself? It was from fear of betraying herself, not from contempt, that she had studied to avoid any intimate conversation at all with him.

The day after the explanation in the garden, Octave visited the Bonnivets' house twice, but Armance did not appear. This singular absence greatly increased his troubled uncertainty about the favourable or fatal result of the step he had allowed himself to take. In the evening he interpreted his cousin's absence as a verdict against him, and lacked courage to distract himself by the sound of empty words; he could not bring himself to speak to anyone at all.

Every time the drawing-room door opened he felt as though his heart were about to break; at last one o'clock struck and it was time to leave. As he left the Bonnivets' house, the hall, the façade, the black marble above the door, the ancient garden wall, all these things seemed to have taken on a peculiar look as a result of Armance's anger. These commonplace objects were endeared to Octave by the melancholy they inspired in him. Dare I say that in his eyes they quickly acquired a kind of tender nobility? He was startled, the following day, when he noticed a likeness between the old garden wall of his house, crowned with a scattering of wallflowers in bloom, and the wall that surrounded the Bonnivets' house.

The third day after that on which he had dared to speak to his cousin, he arrived at Mme de Bonnivet's quite convinced that he was for ever relegated to the rank of mere acquaintance. How boundless was his agitation upon seeing Armance at the piano! She greeted him in a friendly way. He thought her pale and very much altered. And yet he was greatly surprised, and almost restored to a little hope, by the impression that he could discern a certain air of happiness in her eyes.

It was magnificent weather, and Mme de Bonnivet was anxious to take advantage of one of the finest of spring mornings by going for a long drive somewhere. "Will you join us,

66

cousin?" she asked Octave.

"If you please, Madame, unless you're going to the Bois de Boulogne or the Mousseaux." Octave knew that Armance enjoyed neither of these drives.

"Would the Jardin du Roi meet with your approval, if we were to go by the Boulevard?"

"I haven't been there for more than a year."

"And I haven't seen the baby elephant," said Armance, jumping for joy, and away she went to fetch her hat. They set out gaily. Octave was like a different man. Madame de Bonnivet drove past Tortoni's in the barouche with her handsome Octave. So ran the comments of the society gentlemen who caught sight of them. Those who were not in the best of health took the occasion to indulge in dismal reflections upon the fickleness of great ladies who were emulating the manners and behaviour of the court of Louis XV. "In the grave situation towards which we are heading," added these unfortunate people, "it is most ill-advised to surrender the advantages of regular behaviour and decency to the commons and industry. The Jesuits are quite right to be severe from the outset."

Armance mentioned that the bookseller had just sent her three volumes entitled: *History of* ***. "Would you recommend me to read this work?" the Marquise asked Octave. "It's so shamelessly praised in the papers that I mistrust it."

"Nevertheless you'll find it very well-written; the author knows how to tell a story and as yet he has sold himself to no party."

"But is it amusing?" asked Armance.

"As tedious as the plague," replied Octave.

They talked of historical certainty, then of monuments. "Were you not telling me one day recently," enquired Mme de Bonnivet, "that there is nothing certain except monuments?"

"Yes, as regards the history of the Romans and the Greeks, wealthy peoples who did possess monuments; but the libraries are stuffed with thousands of manuscripts about the Middle

Ages, and it's pure laziness on the part of our so-called scholars if we gain no benefit therefrom."

"But those manuscripts are written in such dreadful Latin," argued Mme de Bonnivet.

"Almost unintelligible, maybe, to our scholars, but really not so bad. You would be very pleased with the letters of Héloise to Abelard."

"Their tomb is said to have been in the *Musée Français*, I believe," said Armance. "What has been done with it?"

"It's been put in the Père-Lachaise."

"Let's go and see it," said Mme de Bonnivet, and a few minutes later they reached this English garden, the only one in Paris truly beautiful for its position. They visited Abelard's monument, and Masséna's obelisk; they looked for Labédoyère's tomb. Octave saw the place where young B ✳✳✳ lies buried, and shed some tears for her.

The conversation was serious and solemn, but of moving interest. Feelings ventured to express themselves quite undisguisedly. The only subjects touched upon, in fact, were those unlikely to be compromising, but the celestial charm of candour was none the less keenly appreciable as they strolled along; and here they saw coming towards them a group headed by the witty Comtesse de G ✳✳✳. She came there to seek inspiration, she told Mme de Bonnivet.

This remark almost brought a smile to our friends' lips; never had commonness and affectation seemed so discordant to them. Mme de G ✳✳✳, like all that is vulgar in France, exaggerated her impressions to achieve effect, and the people whose talk she had interrupted toned down their feelings a little as they expressed them, not from dishonesty, but from a kind of instinctive modesty unknown to people without breeding, however intelligent they may be.

After exchanging a few generalities, Octave and Armance found themselves, because of the narrowness of the path, a little way behind:

"You were not well the day before yesterday," said Octave, "and even your friend Méry looked pale as she left your room, which made me fear you might be very ill."

"I wasn't ill at all," replied Armance with slightly forced lightness, "and the interest your long-standing friendship takes in all that concerns me—as Mme de G *** might put it— makes it my duty to acquaint you with the cause of my little sorrows. For some time there has been talk of my marrying; the day before yesterday all the arrangements were on the point of falling through, which was why I was rather upset in the garden. But I beg you to keep this absolutely secret," interposed Armance, startled by a movement of Mme de Bonnivet's as she came back towards them. "I rely on your eternal secrecy, even with your mother, and particularly with my aunt." Octave was exceedingly surprised by this admission, and as Mme de Bonnivet had gone away again he resumed : "Will you allow me to ask you one question; is it solely a marriage of convenience?"

Armance, to whom the exercise and fresh air had imparted a fine colour, all at once turned pale. The day before, as she was laying her heroic plans, she had not foreseen this quite simple question. Octave saw that he had been indiscreet, and was casting about for a pleasantry with which to change the subject, when Armance replied, trying to control her misery : "I hope the person who has been chosen will merit your friendship; he has all mine. But please let us talk no more of this arrangement, which is perhaps still far away." Shortly afterwards they returned to the barouche, and Octave, who found no more to say, asked to be put down at the Gymnase.

CHAPTER IX

Now, peace be here,
Poor house, that keep'st thyself!
Cymbeline

THE NIGHT before, after a day whose horror could only be faintly comprehended by imagining the state of a poor unnerved wretch preparing to undergo a surgical operation of a kind known to be often fatal, an idea had occurred to Armance: "My ties with Octave are close enough for me to be able to tell him that a former friend of my family's is thinking of marrying me. If my tears betrayed me, this disclosure will restore me in his esteem. In the light of this forthcoming marriage and the anxiety it is causing me, my tears will be attributed to some slightly over-pointed allusion to the situation I was in. If he feels a little love for me—alas the day—he will recover from it, but at least I shall be able to remain his friend; I shan't be an exile in a convent, condemned never to see him again, not once, as long as I live."

Armance realized, during the days that followed, that Octave was trying to guess the identity of the person chosen. "He has to know the man in question," she sighed; "my cruel duty extends even to that; only by paying that price may I be allowed to see him again."

She thought of the Baron de Risset, a former leader of the Vendean royalists, a heroic figure who was quite often to be seen in Mme de Bonnivet's drawing-room, though he never uttered a word while he was there.

The very next day Armance spoke to the Baron about the Memoirs of Mme de la Rochejaquelein; she knew he was jealous of them; he proceeded to talk of them at great length and very badly. "Is Mlle de Zohiloff in love with a nephew of the Baron's," wondered Octave, or could it possibly be that the old general's valiant deeds outshine all memory of his fifty-five years? In vain did Octave seek to induce the taciturn baron to conversation; his silence and mistrust were all the greater for finding himself the object of these unwonted attentions.

I know not what exaggerated civility, addressed to Octave by a mother with marriageable daughters, alarmed his misanthropy and caused him to tell his cousin, who was praising the young ladies, that even had they a more eloquent protectress than herself, he, thank God, had forbidden himself all exclusive admiration until the age of twenty-six. This unexpected remark struck Armance like a lightning-flash; never in all her life had she felt so happy. Ten times, perhaps, since his new-found fortune, Octave had spoken in her presence of the time when he should think of marrying. In her surprise at her cousin's remark she realized that she had overlooked this fact.

That moment of happiness was exquisite. The day before, utterly absorbed by the extreme suffering entailed by a great sacrifice for duty's sake, Armance had entirely overlooked this wonderful source of consolation. It was oversights of this kind which caused her to be accused of lack of intelligence by those society people whose hearts' emotions allow them the leisure to notice everything. As Octave was only just twenty, Armance could hope to be his best friend for another six years, and to remain so *with a clear conscience*. "And who knows," she thought to herself, "perhaps I shall be lucky enough to die before those six years are out."

A new page of existence began for Octave. Sanctioned by Armance's show of confidence in him, he would venture to consult her upon the little events of his daily life. Almost every evening he was fortunate enough to be able to talk to her without being exactly overheard by those standing near. He noted with keen pleasure that his confidences, however detailed, were never a burden to her. To lend courage to his reluctance, Armance, too, spoke to him of her sorrows, and a strange and intimate bond grew between the two of them.

The happiest love has its storms; it can even be said to thrive as much upon its terrors as upon its felicities. Neither storms nor anxieties ever troubled the friendship of Armance and Octave. He felt he had no claim on his cousin; there could be no cause for him to complain.

Far from overrating the seriousness of their relationship, these two sensitive beings had never mentioned the subject to each other; even the word friendship had not passed between them since the marriage disclosure beside Abelard's tomb. Although they were for ever seeing each other they could seldom talk without being overheard, and thus, during the brief moments when they were free, they always had so many things to tell each other, so many facts to communicate urgently to each other, that all vain refinement was banished from their conversations.

Unquestionably Octave would have found it difficult to discover a cause for complaint. Every sentiment which the most exalted, the tenderest, the purest love can inspire in the heart of woman, Armance felt for him. The hope of death, which was all the prospect of her love, even lent her language a certain celestial resignation perfectly in keeping with Octave's character.

So keenly did he appreciate the peaceful, perfect happiness with which Armance's gentle friendship filled him, that he hoped he might alter in character.

Since he had made his peace with his cousin he had not relapsed into moments of despair such as that which caused him to regret not having been killed by the carriage which had come galloping out into the Rue de Bourbon. He told his mother: "I am beginning to believe I shall have no more of those crises of fury which used to make you fear for my reason."

Octave was happier, and his mind became clearer. He was surprised to notice many things in society which had never struck him hitherto, though they had been there before his eyes for a long time. The world seemed less hateful, and above all less bent on doing him harm. He told himself that except within the category of devout or ugly women, each person was far more concerned with self, and far less with harming others, than his earlier observation had led him to believe.

He came to recognize that continual frivolity makes all pertinacity impossible; he realized at last that this world, which in his extravagant pride he had believed to be arranged in a manner hostile *to him*, was merely arranged badly. "But such as it is," he said to Armance, "one must take it or leave it. Either one has to end matters swiftly and without hesitation, by using a few drops of prussic acid, or else accept life cheerfully." In speaking thus Octave was seeking to convince himself, much rather than expressing a conviction. His soul was entranced by the happiness he owed to Armance.

His confidences were not always without danger for the young woman. When Octave's reflections took on a sombre hue; when he was unhappy at the prospect of future solitude, Armance was hard put to it to hide from him how wretched it would have made her to picture a moment in her life when she might be separated from him.

"When, at my age, one has no friends," Octave asked her one evening, "can one still hope to acquire any? Can one resolve beforehand to have friends?" Armance, who felt her tears on the brink of betraying her, had to leave him abruptly, saying: "I see my aunt wishes to have a word with me."

Octave, leaning against the window, pursued his sombre train of thought alone. "One mustn't stand aloof from the

73

world," he told himself at last. "It's so wicked that it won't deign to notice that a young man behind a double-locked door on the second floor in the Rue Saint-Dominique hates it passionately. Alas, there's only one person who would notice my absence from the world, and her *friendship* would be deeply wounded by it;" and he began to watch Armance from a distance; she was sitting on her little chair beside the Marquise, and seemed to him at that moment ravishingly beautiful. All Octave's happiness, which he thought so stable and well-secured, nevertheless depended entirely upon that little word *friendship* which he had just pronounced. It is difficult to escape the infirmity of one's century; Octave considered himself philosophical and profound.

All at once Mlle de Zohiloff returned to him looking anxious and almost angry. "An extraordinary slander about you," she said, "has just been related to my aunt. A serious-minded person, someone who has not so far shown any ill-will towards you, came up and told her that often, when you leave here at midnight, you go and end the evening in strange salons which are little more than gaming-houses.

"And that's not all; in these places whose atmosphere is thoroughly degrading you distinguish yourself by excesses which surprise even the oldest habitués. Not only do you find yourself surrounded by women who are a disgrace to the eye, but you talk, you monopolize the conversation. It has even been asserted that you shine in such places with the aid of jests whose bad taste is beyond all belief. People who are interested in you —for there are some even in those salons—first of all did you the honour of assuming that these remarks had been *learnt*. The Vicomte de Malivert is young, they said; he must have observed these jokes being used in some vulgar gathering to stimulate attention and bring a glow of pleasure to the eyes of a few coarse men. But your friends have noticed with sorrow that you have been at pains to invent your most revolting remarks on the spot. In fact the unbelievable scandalousness of your reputed behaviour must have earned you a distressing notoriety among the most ill-bred young men to be found in Paris.

"The person who is slandering you," went on Armance, who was beginning to be a little disconcerted by Octave's obstinate silence, "ended with details which only my aunt's astonishment prevented her from repudiating."

Octave noticed to his delight that Armance's voice trembled throughout this long report. "All that you have been told is true," he said at length, "but it will no longer be so in future. I shall not revisit places where a friend of yours should never have been seen."

Armance' surprise and distress were extreme. For one moment she felt something akin to contempt. But the following day when she saw Octave again, her notion of proper behaviour in a man had undergone a great change. In her cousin's noble confession, and above all in the straightforward undertaking he had given her, she found cause to love him more than ever. Armance thought she was being strict enough with herself in pledging that she would leave Paris and never see Octave again if he revisited those houses so little worthy of him.

CHAPTER X

O conoscenza! non e senza il suo perché
che il fedel prete ti chiamô: il più gran
dei mali. Egli era tutto disturbato, e
però non dubitava ancora, al più al più,
dubitava di esser presto sul punto di
dubitare. O conoscenza! tu sei fatale a
quelli, nei quali l'oprar segue da vicino
il credo.   *Il Cardinal Gerdil*

NEED IT be said that Octave was faithful to his promise?
He gave up pleasures condemned by Armance.

The need to act, and the desire to observe new things had urged him to seek evil company, which is often less tedious than the best. As soon as he was happy a kind of instinct led him to mingle with men; he wished to dominate them.

For the first time Octave had caught a glimpse of the tedium of manners which are too perfect and of the excesses of cold courtesy: bad form allows people to talk at random about themselves, and there is less sense of isolation. When one has served punch in those brilliant salons at the very end of the Rue de Richelieu, which foreigners mistake for the best company, one does not have the sensation of being alone in a desert of humanity. On the contrary, one can believe oneself among twenty intimate friends, not knowing the name of any. Dare we say this at the risk of compromising ourselves and our hero at once? Octave regretted the loss of one or two of his supper-companions.

That part of his life which preceded his close association with the Bonnivet household he was beginning to regard as an era of folly and self-deception. "It was raining," he said to himself in the lively, original way he had; "and instead of taking an umbrella I grew wildly irritated at the condition of the sky, and in moments of enthusiasm for beauty and justice, which were fundamentally no more than fits of madness, I used to imagine that the rain was falling on purpose to do me mischief."

He was delighted to be able to discuss with Mlle de Zohiloff what (like another Philibert) he had observed at various exceedingly elegant balls. "I found an element of unexpectedness there," he told her. "I am no longer so satisfied with the very best of society, which once I loved so much. Beneath a dexterity in conversation it seems to me to suppress all energy, all originality. It accuses of bad manners anyone who does not conform *exactly*. Besides, the best society exceeds its authority. Once it was privileged to judge of what is *correct*; but since it has believed itself attacked it no longer condemns what is coarse and disagreeable without compensation, but rather what it considers harmful to its own interests."

Armance listened coldly to her cousin, and at length she said : "It's only a step from what you are thinking today to jacobinism."

"That would drive me to despair," rejoined Octave sharply.

"Why despair?—at knowing the truth," countered Armance. "Because apparently you would never allow yourself to be converted by a doctrine riddled with falsehood." For the remainder of the evening Octave could not avoid appearing pensive.

Since he had begun to see society a little more in its true colours Octave had suspected that Mme de Bonnivet, for all her supreme pretensions never to give a thought to worldly things and to despise success, was indeed the slave of a boundless ambition.

Certain slanders uttered by the Marquise's enemies, which had chanced to reach him, and which had seemed quite monstrous to him a few months before, now struck him as no more than treacherous or ill-bred exaggerations. "My beautiful cousin is not at all satisfied," he told himself, "with illustrious parentage and immense wealth. Perhaps the splendid existence guaranteed by her blameless conduct, her prudent intelligence and her wise beneficence is a means and not an end for her.

"Mme de Bonnivet needs power. But she is very particular as to the nature of that power. The respect to be gained by high standing in society, by credit at court, by all the advantages one can amass under a monarchy, all this is nothing to her now, for she has enjoyed it too long; it bores her. When one is a king, what is there left? To be God.

"She is surfeited with the pleasures offered by respect from interested motives; she now requires respect from the heart. She has need of the sensation felt by Mahomet when he talks to Seïde, and I have a notion that I came remarkably near the honour of being Seïde.

"My beautiful cousin is lacking in sensibility and so cannot fulfil her life in that way. What she requires is not sublime or touching illusions, not the devotion and passion of one man, but to see herself regarded as a prophetess by a crowd of votaries, and in particular, should one of them rebel, to be able to crush him instantly. She has too positive a character to be content with illusions; she needs the reality of power, and if I go on talking to her open-heartedly about a number of things, that absolute power may one day be wielded at my expense.

"It is inconceivable that she will not soon be besieged by anonymous letters; she will be reproached that I visit her too frequently. The Duchesse d'Ancre, piqued by my neglect of her salon, may well condescend to direct calumny. My favour cannot withstand this double threat. Mme de Bonnivet, while she carefully preserves the outward signs of the warmest friendship, and overwhelms me with reproaches for the infrequency

78

of my visits, will soon compel me to make them very infrequent indeed.

"For instance, I give the impression of being half converted to German mysticism; she'll ask me to undertake publicly some far too ridiculous action. If I agree for the sake of Armance's friendship, something quite impossible will very shortly be suggested to me."

CHAPTER XI

Somewhat light as air.
There's language in her eye, her cheek, her lip,
Nay, her foot speaks; her wanton spirits look out
At every joint and motive of her body.
O these encounteres, so glib of tongue,
That give accosting welcome ere it comes.
Troilus and Cressida, Act IV

THERE WERE few pleasant, society salons, in the circles that visit the king three times a year, which Octave did not enter as a warmly welcomed guest. He observed the renown of Mme la Comtesse d'Aumale. She was the most sparkling coquette—and perhaps the wittiest—of the day. An ill-humoured foreigner has said that the women of high society in France have a turn of mind not unlike that of an aged ambassador. It was a childlike character which sparkled in the behaviour of Mme d'Aumale. Her ingenuous sallies and the madcap gaiety of her actions, invariably prompted by the circumstances of the moment, were the despair of her rivals. Her caprices were so wonderfully unexpected, and how can one imitate a caprice?

Spontaneity and unexpectedness were not the outstanding qualities of Octave's behaviour. His being was compounded of mystery. Heedless he never was, unless it were occasionally in his conversations with Armance. But he needed to be certain that he would not be interrupted unexpectedly. He could not be accused of duplicity; he would have disdained to lie; but he never moved directly towards his object.

Octave took into his service a footman who had been in Mme d'Aumale's employ; this man, an old soldier, was self-seeking and very shrewd. Octave took him out riding, long seven or eight league rides through the woods around Paris, and there were moments of apparent boredom when he would allow the man to talk to him. Within a few weeks Octave was in possession of the most reliable information concerning Mme d'Aumale's conduct. The young woman, who had gravely compromised herself by her unbounded thoughtlessness, in reality deserved all the esteem which she was no longer accorded by certain people.

Octave assessed the amount of time and care that Mme d'Aumale's company would demand of him, and he hoped that he could soon, without too much inconvenience, pass for that brilliant woman's lover. So well did he arrange matters that it was Mme de Bonnivet herself, in the course of a party she was giving at her château at Andilly, who presented him to Mme d'Aumale; and in picturesque circumstances, impressive to the heedless young Comtesse.

With the intention of enlivening a nocturnal walk they were taking through the delightful woods that crown the heights of Andilly, Octave suddenly appeared disguised as a magician, and illuminated by a number of Bengal lights cunningly hidden behind some of the old tree-trunks. Octave was looking very handsome that evening, and Mme de Bonnivet, without realizing it herself, spoke of him with a kind of rapture. Less than a month after this first encounter, people were beginning to say that the Vicomte de Malivert had succeeded M. de R *** and so many others, in the post of intimate friend to Mme d'Aumale.

This woman, who was so frivolous that neither she nor any-one else ever knew what she would be doing a quarter of an hour later, had noticed that a drawing-room clock chiming midnight sends home most of the bores, people of regular habits; so she used to entertain from midnight until two o'clock.

81

Octave was always the last to leave Mme de Bonnivet's drawing-room, when he would drive his horses to death in order to arrive the sooner at Mme d'Aumale's house in the Chaussée d'Antin. Here he would find a woman who thanked heaven for her high birth and riches, solely because they allowed her the privilege of indulging every passing caprice the whole day through.

At a country house, at midnight, when everyone leaves the drawing-room, if Mme d'Aumale happened to notice as she crossed the hall that the moonlight was pleasantly soft and mild, she would take the arm of whichever young man seemed most amusing that night, and away she would go through the woods. If some fool offered to accompany her on her walk she would beg him unceremoniously to go off in the opposite direction; but the following day, if her escort of the night before had bored her at all, she would not speak to him again. It must be admitted that it was extremely difficult, in the company of so quick a wit—at the command of so unruly a disposition—not to appear a little dull.

This was where Octave came into his own; the amusing element in his character was quite invisible to those who, before they act, always think of a pattern to follow and of conventions to be observed. No one, on the other hand, was likely to be more aware of it than the prettiest woman in Paris, for ever running after some new idea that might help her spend a stimulating evening. Octave followed Mme d'Aumale wherever she went, for example to the Théâtre Italien.

During Mme Pasta's last two or three performances, whither the fashion had drawn all Paris, he was at pains to talk very loudly to the young Comtesse, in such a way as to disturb the whole theatre. Mme d'Aumale, amused by what he was telling her, was overjoyed by the air of artlessness he maintained while he was being impertinent.

To Octave, nothing seemed to be in worse taste; but he was beginning to carry off stupidities not at all badly. When he indulged in some absurdity, the double attention he paid, despite himself, to his impertinence and to the sensible behaviour the occasion really demanded, lent his eyes a certain fire which amused Mme d'Aumale. Octave found it pleasing to have it rumoured everywhere that he was madly in love with the Comtesse, and yet never to say to this delightful young woman, with whom he spent all his time, anything even remotely connected with love.

Mme de Malivert, surprised at her son's behaviour, occasionally visited the salons where he was to be found in the wake of Mme d'Aumale. One evening, as she was taking leave of Mme de Bonnivet, she begged her for the loan of Armance the following day. "I have a great many papers to set in order, and need my Armance's sharp eyes."

The next day, as agreed, Mme de Malivert's carriage called for Armance as early as eleven o'clock, before the midday meal. The two ladies lunched alone. When Mme de Malivert's maid withdrew, her mistress warned her: "Remember, I am at home to no one; no more to Octave than to M. de Malivert." She even took the precaution of locking the ante-room door herself.

When she was comfortably settled in her armchair, with Armance seated before her on her little chair: "My child," she said to her, "I am going to speak to you of something about which I made up my mind a long time ago. You have no more than a hundred louis a year: that's all my enemies will be able to say against my passionate wish that you should marry my son." With these words Mme de Malivert threw herself into Armance's arms. It was the poor girl's finest hour; sweet tears streamed down her face.

CHAPTER XII

Estavas, linda Ignez, posta em socego
De teus annos colhendo doce fruto
Naquelle engano da alma ledo e cego
Que a fortuna, naô deixa durar muito.
Os Lusiadas, Canto III

"**B**UT MOTHER dearest," said Armance much later, when they had somewhat regained the power of rational speech, "Octave has never mentioned that he had any attachment for me such as I feel a husband ought to have for his wife." "If I did not have to stand up to lead you to a looking-glass," replied Mme de Malivert, "I should show you your eyes shining with happiness at this moment, and then beg you to tell me once again that you are not sure of Octave's heart. I am sure of it myself, and I am only his mother. Moreover I am not by any means blind to the possible shortcomings of my son, and I don't want you to give me your answer before a full week is out."

I do not know whether it was the effect of the Sarmatian blood running in her veins, or of her premature misfortunes, but Armance possessed the faculty of perceiving at a glance all the possible consequences implicit in any sudden altering of life. And whether her own fate, or that of some unimportant outsider, depended on this new pattern of things, she could foresee the results with equal clarity. This strength of character or of mind earned her both the everyday confidences and the rebukes of Mme de Bonnivet. The Marquise readily consulted her about her most intimate plans; yet at other times she would tell her: "With a mind like that a girl is never quite as she should be."

After the first instant of happiness and deep gratitude, it occurred to Armance that she should say nothing to Mme de Malivert about the untrue story she had confided to Octave concerning her supposed marriage. "Mme de Malivert has not consulted her son," she thought, "or else he has concealed from her the obstacle which stands in the way of her plan." This second possibility cast a dark shadow over Armance's heart.

She wanted to believe that Octave felt no love for her; day after day she needed to be certain of this, to justify in her own eyes the many thoughtful attentions her fond friendship indulged in, and yet this terrible proof of her cousin's indifference, suddenly presented to her, crushed her beneath an enormous burden, and bereft her even of the power of speech.

What sacrifices would Armance not have made at that moment to win the opportunity of weeping without restraint! "If Octave's mother detects tears in my eyes," she thought, "heaven knows what decisive conclusions she may feel justified in drawing. Who knows but that in her eagerness for this match she may mention those tears to her son as proof that I am responsive to his alleged tenderness?" Mme de Malivert was not at all surprised by the deeply pensive expression Armance assumed towards the end of her day's visit.

The two ladies returned to the Bonnivets' together, and although Armance had not seen her cousin all day, even his presence, when she caught sight of him in the drawing-room, was powerless to dispel her dark mood of sadness. She barely answered him; she had not strength enough to do so. Her preoccupation became evident to Octave, no less than her lack of response to him; and he said to her sadly: "You have no time today to consider that I am your friend."

Armance's only reply was to gaze fixedly at him, and though

she did not realize it her eyes took on that deep, solemn expression that occasioned her aunt to deliver such high-sounding lectures to her.

Octave's remark pierced her to the heart; so he was unaware, then, of his mother's action, or more probably had no interest in it, and only wished to be a friend. After she had watched the guests leave, and had heard out Mme de Bonnivet's confidences upon the state of all her various plans, when Armance was at last able to be alone in her little room, she fell a prey to the most dismal grief. Never had she felt so unhappy; to be alive had never hurt her so much. How bitterly she regretted the romances into which she sometimes allowed her imagination to wander! In those happy moments she would dare to say: "If I had been born rich, and Octave had been able to choose me as his life's companion, given the character I know he possesses, he would have found more happiness with me than with any other woman on earth."

Now she was paying dearly for this dangerous make-believe. Armance's sorrow grew no less deep in the days that followed; not for a moment could she abandon herself to day-dreaming, without becoming utterly weary of everything, and she had the misfortune to feel her position keenly. The extraneous obstacles in the way of a marriage to which, in any event, she would never have agreed seemed to be vanishing; but Octave's heart alone was not for her.

Mme de Malivert, having witnessed the beginnings of her son's passion for Armance, had been alarmed by his assiduous attentions to the brilliant Comtesse d'Aumale. But no sooner had she seen them together than she was able to guess that the relationship was a duty her son had imposed upon himself, in his peculiar way; Mme de Malivert well knew that if she questioned him about it he would tell her the truth; but she had studiously abstained from even the most indirect enquiries. Her rights, she felt, did not extend so far as that. In deference to what she believed she owed to the dignity of her sex, she had wished to speak of the match to Armance before discussing it with her son, of whose passion she was certain.

When she had announced her intention to Mlle de Zohiloff, Mme de Malivert contrived to spend hours on end in Mme de Bonnivet's drawing-room. She thought she noticed that something strange was going on between Armance and her son. Clearly Armance was very unhappy. "Could it possibly be," wondered Mme de Malivert, "that Octave, who adores her and sees her constantly, has never told her he loves her?"

The day had arrived when Mlle de Zohiloff was to give her answer. In the morning Mme de Malivert sent her carriage round for her early, and a little note in which she invited Armance to come and spend an hour with her. Armance arrived, looking as people do after a long illness; she would not have had the strength to come round on foot. As soon as she was alone with Mme de Malivert she said to her in a perfectly gentle manner, within which could be glimpsed the resolution that springs from despair : "My cousin's character is full of originality; his happiness, and maybe mine too," she added, blushing scarlet, "require that my sweet mother shall never mention a word to him of a plan inspired by her very great prejudice in my favour." Mme de Malivert affected to give her consent very reluctantly to what she was being asked. "I may die sooner than I expect," she told Armance, "and then my son will not win the only woman on earth who can soothe the un-happiness of his character." "I am sure your decision is based on the question of money," she told her another time; "Octave, who is for ever telling you some secret or other, has not been so misguided as to fail to confess something of which I am positive, that is that he loves you with all the passion he is capable of; and that's saying a good deal, my child. And if certain spells of over-excitement, which grow less frequent as the days go by, should raise any objections against the character of the hus-band I am offering you, you will nevertheless know the sweet-ness of being loved as few women are nowadays. In the stormy

87

times which may be to come, strength of character in a man will mean a strong probability of happiness for his family.

"You yourself know, Armance my dear, that the external obstacles which crush ordinary men are nothing to Octave. If his soul is at peace with itself, the whole world in league against him would not cause him a quarter of an hour's sadness. Now I am quite certain that his peace of mind depends on your consent. Conclude for yourself how fervently I must entreat for it; my son's happiness depends on you. For four years I have been thinking day and night of some means to ensure it, and could not discover one; now at last he has come to love you. As for me, I shall fall victim to your excessive delicacy of feeling. You do not wish to be blamed for marrying a husband much richer than yourself, and I shall carry to my grave the keenest anxiety about Octave's future, without having seen my son wedded to the woman who, in my lifetime, I have esteemed most of all."

These assurances of Octave's love were heartrending to Armance. Mme de Malivert noticed an undercurrent of irritation and hurt pride in the replies of her young relative. That evening, at Mme de Bonnivet's, she observed that her son's presence did nothing to allay in Mlle de Zohiloff that kind of unhappiness which results from fear of having shown insufficient pride towards the loved one, and so perhaps having lost some of his esteem. "Certainly a poor girl without family," thought Armance, "ought never to forget herself in that way."

Mme de Malivert herself was very uneasy. After many sleepless nights, she at length reached a conclusion—a strange one, yet likely in view of her son's peculiar character—that indeed, just as Armance had said, he had not spoken to her at all of his love.

"Is it possible," thought Mme de Malivert, "that Octave should be so timid? He loves his cousin; she is the one person in the world who can guard him against those fits of melancholy which have made me tremble for him."

88

After thinking it over a great deal, she made her decision; one day she said casually enough to Armance : "I don't know what you have done to my son to discourage him; but while he confesses that he is deeply attached to you and holds you in the most perfect esteem, and that to obtain your hand would be the greatest good fortune in his eyes, he adds that you raise an insuperable barrier against his dearest wishes, and that he would certainly not wish to win you as a result of our persecuting you into accepting him."

CHAPTER XIII

Ay! que ya siento en mi cuidoso pecho
Labrarme poco a poco un vivo fuego
Y desde alli con movimiento blando
Ir por venas y huesos penetrando.
Araucana, c. XXII

T HE EXTREME happiness which showed itself in Armance's
eyes consoled Mme de Malivert, who indeed felt somewhat remorseful at employing a little untruth in so
serious a negotiation. "After all," she said to herself, "what
harm can there be in hastening on the marriage of two children
who are charming, though a trifle proud, and who feel a passion
for each other such as is seldom seen in this world. Is not my
first duty to preserve my son's reason?"

The curious decision Mme de Malivert had just taken had
rescued Armance from the deepest sorrow she had ever experienced in her life. A little earlier she had wished for death, and
this remark, supposedly made by Octave, set her upon a pinnacle of bliss. She was quite determined never to accept her
cousin's hand; but this delightful remark allowed her once
again to entertain the hope of many years of happiness. "I can
love him secretly," she said to herself, "during the six years
until his marriage, and I shall be just as happy as if I were his
wife—perhaps much happier. It is said, isn't it, that marriage
is the tomb of love, and that while there can be pleasant mar-
riages, there are none truly delightful? I tremble at the thought
of marrying my cousin. If I were ever to see that he was not the

happiest man on earth I should myself fall to the depths of despair. On the other hand, if we live in pure and saintly friendship, none of the petty self-interest in life will ever reach up to our lofty sentiments and so blight them."

With all the calm of happiness, Armance pondered the reasons she had once given herself for never accepting Octave's hand. "In the eyes of the world I should be a lady companion who has seduced the son of the house. Even now I can hear the comments of Mme la Duchesse d'Ancre, and even of the most respectable women, such as the Marquise de Seyssins, who sees in Octave a husband for one of her daughters.

"The loss of my reputation would be all the swifter because I have lived on intimate terms with several women of the highest standing in Paris. They can say anything about me, and they will be believed. Heavens, into what an abyss of shame they can hurl me! And I could very well lose Octave's esteem one day, for I have no means of defending myself. In what drawing-room could I make myself heard? Where are my friends? And besides, in terms of the obvious baseness of such an action, what possible justification could there be? If I had a family, a brother, a father, would they ever believe that, were Octave in my place and I the very wealthy one, I should be as devoted to him as I am at this moment?"

Armance had a reason for feeling keenly about indelicacy in money matters. Only a very few days before, Octave had said to her, apropos a certain majority vote which had caused a stir: "I hope that when I have taken my place in public life I shall not allow myself to be bought as these gentlemen are. I can live on five francs a day, and under an assumed name I'm capable of earning twice that sum in any country as a chemist attached to some manufacturing house."

Armance was so happy that she did not refrain from examining any objection, however perilous the airing of it might be. "If Octave were to prefer me to the wealth and influence he could expect from the family of a wife who was his equal in

91

rank, we could go and live in solitude together. Why shouldn't we spend ten months of the year in that lovely Malivert estate, in Dauphiné, about which he often tells me? Society would very quickly forget us. Yes, but I should not forget that there is one place on earth where I am despised, and despised by the noblest souls.

"To see love wane to nothing in the heart of an adored husband is the greatest misfortune that can befall a young woman born wealthy. And yet such a dreadful misfortune would be a mere nothing to me. Even if he were to continue to cherish me, every day would be poisoned by the fear that Octave might come to believe that I had chosen him because of the difference in our fortunes. This idea would not occur to him spontaneously—that I will believe—anonymous letters, like those which are addressed to Mme de Bonnivet, would lay it before his eyes. I should tremble at every package that arrived by the post. No, whatever happens, I must never accept Octave's hand, and the road that honour bids me take is the safest way to our happiness."

On the day after the one which had been so happy for Armance, Mme de Malivert and Mme de Bonnivet moved out to a pretty château hidden among the woods that crown the heights of Andilly. Mme de Malivert's doctors had prescribed riding and walking for her, and the very next day after her arrival at Andilly, she decided to try out two handsome little ponies which she had ordered from Scotland for Armance and herself. Octave accompanied the two ladies on their first ride. Hardly had they covered a quarter of a league when he began to sense rather more reserve in his cousin's behaviour towards him, and in particular a marked tendency to be gay.

This discovery gave him much food for thought, and what he observed during the remainder of the ride confirmed his suspicions. Armance was no longer the same for him. It was clear that she was about to be married; he was going to lose the only friend he had in the world. As he helped Armance to dismount he contrived to say to her, without being overheard by Mme de Malivert: "I am very much afraid my pretty cousin will soon be changing her name; when this happens it will rob me of the only person in the world who has been kind enough to grant me a measure of friendship." "NEVER," replied Armance, "will I cease to feel the most devoted and exclusive friendship for you." But even as she spoke these hurried words there was such happiness in her eyes that Octave, predisposed, saw there the realization of all his fears.

The kindness, the air of intimacy, as it were, with which Armance treated him during the excursion the next day, bereft him of any remaining peace of mind "I can see a decided change in Mlle de Zohiloff's behaviour," he said to himself; "a few days ago she was exceedingly agitated, and now she is exceedingly happy. I have no idea what has caused the change; therefore it can only be to my disadvantage.

"How could anyone be so foolish as to choose a girl of eighteen for an intimate friend? She gets married, and that's the end of it. It's because of my damnable pride that I would rather die a thousand deaths than dare to tell a man the things I confide to Mlle de Zohiloff.

"To work would be one solution; but have I not abandoned all reasonable occupations? To tell the truth, hasn't my only work for the last six months been the endeavour to make myself agreeable to a society both selfish and dull?" To engage at least in this kind of useful inconvenience, Octave would leave Andilly when his mother's excursion was over, and go to pay calls in Paris. He was looking for new habits to fill the void which his charming cousin would create in his life when she parted company with him to follow her husband; the idea of this spurred him to need violent exercise.

The more his heart was constricted with sadness, the more he talked and sought to please; what he dreaded was to be alone with himself, and most of all the prospect of the future. He was for ever repeating to himself: "I was a child to choose a mere girl as a friend." This remark, by its very obviousness, he soon came to regard as a kind of proverb, and it prevented him from pursuing his researches deeper into his own heart.

Armance, who saw that he was sad, was much moved, and frequently blamed herself for the untrue story she had confided to him. Never a day went by but she was tempted, as she saw him leaving for Paris, to tell him the truth. "But that lie is my only strength against him," she told herself; "if I once confess that I am not plighted, he will beg me to yield to his mother's wishes, and how could I then resist? No, I must never consent under any pretext; that alleged marriage to a stranger is my only defence against a happiness that would ruin us both."

To dispel her too dear cousin's sadness Armance, when she was with him, allowed herself all the little pleasantries that belong to the tenderest friendship. There was such grace and naïve gaiety in the girl's assurances of eternal friendship—she who was so natural in all she did—that Octave's black misanthropy often gave way before them. He would be happy in spite of himself; and at these times, too, nothing was wanting to complete Armance's happiness.

"How sweet it is," she would tell herself, "to do one's duty! Supposing that I, a poor girl with no family, were Octave's wife, should I be as content? I should be constantly beset by a thousand cruel suspicions." But after these occasions when she was so pleased with herself and with others, Armance always ended by treating Octave better than she would have wished. She watched her words carefully, and her words never expressed anything beyond the purest friendship. But the tone of voice in which certain things were spoken! The glances which sometimes went with them! Anyone but Octave would have recognized in them the lineaments of the keenest passion. He enjoyed them without understanding them.

When he could think uninterruptedly of his cousin, his thoughts would no longer bestow passion on anything else in the world. He became fair again, and even indulgent; and his happiness led him to abandon his strictures upon a number of subjects: he now regarded fools merely as beings of unfortunate parentage.

"Is a man to blame if he has black hair?" he said to Armance. "But it's up to me to avoid that man carefully if the colour of his hair offends me."

In some circles Octave was thought ill-natured, and fools were instinctively afraid of him; at this period they reconciled themselves with him. He often carried with him into society all the happiness he owed to Armance. He was less feared; his good-nature was considered more youthful. It must be confessed that all his actions contained an element of the intoxication deriving from the kind of happiness that one does not admit to oneself; life flowed swiftly and exquisitely by for him. His thoughts about himself no longer bore the stamp of that inexorable logic, harsh and glorying in its harshness, which had directed all his actions in earlier youth. Now that he often began a sentence without knowing how he would finish it, he spoke a great deal better.

CHAPTER XIV

*Il giovin cuore o non vede affatto i difetti
di chi li sta vicino o li vede immensi. Error
commune ai giovinetti che portono fuoco nell'
interno dell' anima.*   *Lampugnani*

ONE DAY Octave heard in Paris that a man whom he
used to see more often and with greater pleasure than
most, one of his friends, as society would call it, owed
the fine fortune which he was spending so graciously, to
what Octave regarded as the basest of all actions (a mis-
appropriated inheritance). Mlle de Zohiloff, to whom he
hastened on his arrival at Andilly to impart this vexatious
discovery, decided that he bore it remarkably well. There was
no misanthropic outburst, and he showed no desire to break
with the man insultingly.

Another day he returned very early from a château in
Picardy where he was to have spent the whole evening. "How
dreadfully insipid those conversations are," he told Armance.
"Nothing but hunting, the beauty of the countryside, Rossini's
music, the Arts! Moreover the interest they take in these things
is in itself a lie. People like that are stupid enough to be afraid;
they believe themselves to be in a beleaguered town and forbid
themselves to speak of the siege. What a miserable species—
and how cross I am that I belong to it."

"Well," said Armance, "go and have a look at the besiegers;
their ludicrousness will help you bear that of the army in whose

96

ranks you happen to have been born."

"This is a serious problem," said Octave. "God knows, I suffer when, in one of our salons, I hear one of our friends putting forward an opinion which is either absurd or cruel, but at least I can preserve an honourable silence. My anguish is entirely invisible. But if I am introduced to Martigny the banker. . . ."

"Well," Armance interrupted, "that man, so shrewd, so witty, such a slave to his vanity, will welcome you with open arms."

"No doubt; but for my part, however moderate, however modest, however silent I may try to be, I shall end by expressing my opinion on something or somebody. A moment later the drawing-room door will open with a great commotion; Mr. So-and-so, the manufacturer from * * * will be announced, and will shout from the doorway in stentorian tones : 'Would you believe it, my dear Martigny, there are ultras stupid enough, dull enough, witless enough to say that . . .' And thereupon the good manufacturer will repeat word for word the very scrap of opinion which I have that moment uttered in all modesty. What can I do?"

"Fail to hear."

"That's what I would be inclined to do. I am not on this earth to set right coarse manners or crooked minds; even less do I wish to give this man, by talking to him, the right to shake hands with me when he meets me in the street. But in that drawing-room I have the misfortune not to be exactly like everyone else. Would to God I could find there the *equality* about which these gentlemen make such a fuss! For instance, what do you suppose I can do about the title I bear, when I am announced at M. Martigny's?"

"But you intend to give up your title if ever you can without scandalizing your father."

"Certainly; but would not the omission of that title, as I gave my name to M. Martigny's footman, look like an act of cowardice? It's like Rousseau calling his dog *Turc* instead of *Duc* because there was a duke present in the room."*

"But they don't hate titles so much in the liberal bankers' houses," said Armance; "the other day Mme de Claix, who goes everywhere, was at M. Montange's ball, and you know very well that in the evening she made us all laugh by claiming that they're so fond of titles that she had heard the announcement: *Madame la colonelle....*"

"Since the steam engine became queen of the world, a title has been an absurdity, but when all's said and done, here am I all tricked out in that absurdity. If I don't uphold it, it will crush me. The title draws attention to me. If I don't reply to that manufacturer's thunderous voice when he shouts from the door that what I have just said is nonsense, won't a few glances search me out? This is the weakness in my character: I can't toss my head and make light of everything, as Mme d'Aumale would have it. If I perceive those glances, all pleasure is going to desert me for the rest of the evening. The discussion which will be set in motion within me, to establish whether I have been deliberately insulted, may banish my peace of mind for three days."

"But are you quite certain," said Armance, "of this alleged coarseness of manners with which you so generously endow the opposing faction? Didn't you see the other day that Talma's children and the sons of a duke are being brought up together in the same boarding-school?"

"It's the men of forty-five, who grew rich during the Revo-

* Like Rousseau, poor Octave is striving against shadows. He would have passed unnoticed in every salon in Paris, despite the word that precedes his name. Besides, in his portrayal of the section of society he has never seen there is an absurd note of animosity, of which he is later to rid himself. Fools belong to all classes. If any one class were to be rightly or wrongly accused of coarseness, it would soon become conspicuous for its great prudishness and solemnity of behaviour.

lution, that monopolize the conversation in the salons—not the playmates of Talma's children."

"I'll wager they're wittier than many of our people. Who in the Chamber of Peers is brilliant? The other day you were remarking on it sorrowfully yourself."

"Ah, if only I were still giving my pretty cousin lessons in logic, how I should laugh at her! What does a man's wit matter to me?—his manners are what can fill me with sadness. The biggest fool among our people, M. de *** for example, may be exceedingly ridiculous, but he is never offensive. The other day at the d'Aumales' I was describing my little trip to Liancourt, and speaking of the latest machinery that the good duke has had sent from Manchester. A man who was present suddenly said: *'That's not it; that's not true.'* I was satisfied that he did not wish to give me the lie; but the coarseness of it left me speechless for an hour."

"And was this man a banker?"

"He wasn't one of us. The amusing part is that I wrote to the foreman of the carding-house at Liancourt, and it turns out that my contradictious fellow wasn't even right."

"I don't notice that M. Montange, the young banker who comes to visit Mme de Claix, has uncouth manners."

"He has sugary ones, and when uncouth manners are afraid, that is what they turn into."

"I think their wives look very pretty," pursued Armance. "I should like to find out if their conversation is spoilt by that tinge of hatred or of dignity on its guard, which is sometimes manifest among us. Oh, how I wish a good judge like my cousin could tell me what goes on in those drawing-rooms! When I see the bankers' ladies in their boxes at the Théâtre Italien, I would give anything to hear what they say among themselves, and to join in their conversation. When I see one who is pretty —and there are some charming ones amongst them—I would give anything to fling my arms round her neck. All this will seem very childish to you; but I have this to say to you, Sir

99

Philosopher, the expert in logic : How can you know mankind if you observe only one class? And the least energetic class at that, since it is the furthest removed from the needs of reality!"

"And the class with the most affectation, since it believes itself to be observed. You must admit it's a good thing for a philosopher to provide arguments for his opponent," said Octave laughing. "Would you believe it, yesterday at the Saint-Imiers', M. le Marquis de * * *, who was making such fun here the other day of little newspapers of whose very existence he disclaimed all knowledge, was in the seventh heaven because *l'Aurore* has published a filthy joke against his enemy M. le Comte de * * *, who has just been made a Councillor of State? He had a copy in his pocket."

"It's one of the misfortunes of our position to see fools telling the most ridiculous lies, yet not to dare say to them : 'A fine disguise, but I recognize you!' "

"We have to do without the funniest jokes, because they might make the other party laugh if they heard them."

"I am acquainted with bankers only through our smooth-tongued Montange," said Armance, "and also through that delightful comedy *le Roman*; but I doubt whether, when it comes to worshipping money, they can do more than hold their own with certain of our people. It's very hard, believe me, to undertake the perfecting of a whole class. I shan't speak to you any more of the pleasure it would give me to hear news of these ladies. But as the old Duc de * * * used to say in Petersburg, when he had the *Journal de l'Empire* sent to him at such great expense, and at the risk of scandalizing the Emperor Alexander : 'Don't you think one ought to read the memoirs of the opposing party?' "

"*Je vous dirai bien plus, mais avec confidence,* as Talma says so beautifully in *Polyeucte* : at bottom, you and I certainly don't want to live with these people; but on many questions we think as they do."

"And it's sad at our age," continued Armance, "to make

up our minds to be on the losing side all our lives."

"We're like the priests of the idols of paganism, at the time when the Christian religion was about to sweep it away. Today we are still the persecutors; we still have the police and the budget on our side; but tomorrow perhaps, we shall ourselves be persecuted by public opinion."

"You do us a great deal of honour in comparing us with those good pagan priests. I see something more false in our position, yours and mine. We only belong to this party to share in its misfortunes."

"It's only too true; we see its absurdities without daring to laugh at them, and its advantages we find a burden. What do I care how ancient my name is? I should have to violate my scruples to take advantage of it."

"The conversation of young people of your own sort sometimes makes you want to shrug your shoulders, and lest you yield to this temptation you hasten to speak of Mlle de Claix's beautiful sketchbook or Mme Pasta's singing. On the other hand, your title, and their perhaps somewhat unpolished behaviour, prevent you from seeing the people who think as you do upon three quarters of all questions."

"Ah, how I wish I were in command of a big gun or a steam engine! How happy I should be as a chemist working for some manufacturing house; for roughness of manners matters little to me—one grows accustomed to it in a week."

"Besides which you're not so sure they are as rough as all that," said Armance.

"Even were they ten times rougher," pursued Octave, "there is in this all the fun of *acting* the foreign tongue; but one would have to call oneself M. Martin or M. Lenoir."

"Couldn't you find a sensible man who has conducted a campaign of discovery in the liberal salons?"

"Several of my friends go there to dance; they say that the ices are perfect there, and that's all. One of these fine days I shall risk going myself, for there's nothing more idiotic than to spend a year on end wondering about a danger which perhaps doesn't exist."

In the end Armance made him confess that he had thought of a way of appearing in the circles to which wealth, and not birth, gives entry: "Well, yes, I have found a way," said Octave, "but the cure would be worse than the disease, because it would cost me several months of my life, which I should be obliged to spend away from Paris."

"What is the way?" asked Armance, grown suddenly very serious.

"I should go to London, and there, naturally, I should meet everyone of distinction in high society. How could I go to England without arranging to be introduced to the Marquess of Lansdowne, to Mr. Brougham, to Lord Holland? These gentlemen will speak to me of our famous men in France; they will be surprised to find that I am not acquainted with them; I shall express deep regret at this, and when I come back I shall arrange to be introduced to everyone of note in France. This move, if they do me the honour of discussing it at the Duchesse d'Ancre's, will in no way seem a betrayal of the ideas that might be thought inseparable from my name; it will simply be the very natural desire to know the great people of the century we live in. I shall never forgive myself for not having met M. le Général Foy."

Armance said nothing.

"Isn't it a humiliating thing," continued Octave, "that all who support us, even the *monarchist* writers whose task it is to preach every morning in the paper about the advantages of birth and of religion, should be supplied to us by the class that has all the advantages, except birth!"

"Oh, if M. de Soubirane were to hear you...."

"Don't attack me upon the greatest of my misfortunes, that of having to lie all day long...."

The tenor of perfect intimacy will tolerate parentheses ad infinitum, which are pleasing because they give proof of a boundless confidence, though they may very well be tedious to a third party. It is sufficient that we have indicated that the Vicomte de Malivert's brilliant position was far from being a source of unmixed pleasure to him.

It is not without some danger that we shall have been faithful historians. If politics cuts across such a simple narrative it may produce the effect of a pistol shot in the middle of a concert. Besides, Octave is by no means a philosopher, and has been very unfair in his characterization of the two faint differences which divided society in his time. How scandalous that Octave shouldn't reason like a sage of fifty !*

* We are not grateful enough to the Villèle government. The three per cent, the Law of Primogeniture, the Press laws, have brought about a fusion of the parties. The dealings necessary between Peers and Deputies have been the first step in this reconciliation which Octave could not foresee, and fortunately the ideas of this proud, shy young man are even less correct today than they were a few months ago; but that is the way he must have seen things, given the character he had. Would it have been right for the sketch of a strange character to be left incomplete merely because he is unfair to everybody? It is precisely this unfairness which is his misfortune.

CHAPTER XV

How am I glutted with conceit of this!
Shall I make spirits fetch me what I please?
Resolve me of all ambiguities?
Perform what desperate enterprise I will?
Doctor Faustus

S o OFTEN did Octave leave Andilly to go and see Mme
d'Aumale in Paris that some slight feelings of jealousy
one day overcast Armance's gaiety. When her cousin
returned in the evening she asserted her sovereignty. "Will you
oblige Madame your mother on one point which she will never
mention to you?"

"Certainly."

"Well then, for three months—that's to say for ninety days
—don't refuse an invitation to a ball, and never leave a ball
until after you have danced."

"I should prefer a fortnight under arrest," said Octave.

"You're not hard to please," rejoined Armance, "but do
you promise, or not?"

"I promise everything, except the three months' constancy.
Since I'm the victim of tyranny here," Octave laughed, "I
shall desert. There's an old idea of mine which, despite myself,
preoccupied me the whole of yesterday evening at M. de * * *'s
magnificent party, where I danced as though I had guessed
your orders. If I were to leave Andilly for six months, I have
two plans more amusing than that of going to England.

"The first is to adopt the name of M. Lenoir; under this fine

104

alias I should go into the provinces and give lessons in arithmetic, in geometry as applied to the arts, in anything you like. I should go by way of Bourges, Aurillac, Cahors; I should easily obtain letters from several peers, members of the Institute, who would recommend M. Lenoir to the Prefects as a scholar, royalist, etc.

"But the other plan is a better one. As a schoolmaster I should see only keen, fickle little schoolboys who would soon bore me, and a few parish intrigues.

"I hesitate to confide the finest of my plans to you : I should take the name of Pierre Gerlat, and, starting off in Geneva or Lyon I should arrange to become the manservant of some young man destined to play more or less the same role as myself in the world. Pierre Gerlat would be the bearer of excellent references from the Vicomte de Malivert, whom he would have served faithfully for six years. In a word, I should adopt the name and the existence of poor Pierre whom I once threw out of the window. Two or three of my acquaintances will accommodate me with references. They will seal them with their coats-of-arms upon enormous lumps of sealing-wax, and in this way I hope to obtain a place with some young Englishman, a very rich one, or the son of a peer. I shall be careful to spoil my hands with a diluted acid. I've learned how to black boots from my present servant, my brave corporal Voreppe. For the last three months I've been stealing all his talents from him."

"One evening your master will come home drunk and kick Pierre Gerlat."

"Even if he throws me out of the window, I have foreseen that objection. I shall defend myself, and the following day give in my notice, and bear him no ill-will."

"You would become guilty of a culpable abuse of confidence. One may allow one's faults of character to be seen by a young peasant who is quite incapable of understanding one's most peculiar traits, but I think one would take great care not to behave so before a man of one's own class."

105

"I should never relate what I had discovered. Besides, a *master*, as Pierre Gerlat would say, runs a grave risk of *happening* upon a rogue; this one's man will be no more than inquisitive. Understand my difficulties," pursued Octave. "My imagination is so foolish at certain times, and so greatly exaggerates what I owe to my position, that although I am no sovereign I yearn for *incognito*. I am a sovereign by virtue of misfortune, of ridicule, of the extreme importance I attach to certain things. I feel an imperious need to see another Vicomte de Malivert in action. Since unfortunately I have embarked on this role—since to my great and sincere regret I cannot be the son of the senior foreman at M. de Liancourt's carding factory, I need six months' domestic service to cure the Vicomte de Malivert of several of his weaknesses.

"This is the only way; my pride sets a wall of diamond between me and the rest of mankind. Your presence, my dear cousin, causes this diamond wall to vanish. In your presence I should never take anything amiss, but by mischance I have no magic carpet to take you here, there and everywhere. I cannot see you as a third person when I go riding in the Bois de Boulogne with one of my *friends*. There's not one of them who, very soon after we first become acquainted, is not *hounded* from me by my conversation. When at last, a year later, and very much against my will, they understand me completely, they wrap themselves about with the strictest reserve and would, I believe, prefer their most intimate thoughts and actions to be known to the devil rather than to me. I shouldn't like to swear that several of them don't indeed take me for *Lucifer himself*, as M. de Soubirane will have it in one of his witticisms, *come upon earth expressly to disquiet them*."

Octave was explaining these strange ideas to his cousin as they walked in the Montlignon woods, a little apart from Mme de Bonnivet and Mme de Malivert. His fancies preoccupied Armance a great deal. The next day, when her cousin had left for Paris, her free and lively air, which often verged upon the extravagant, gave place to those tender fixed looks from which Octave could not avert his glance when he was present.

Mme de Bonnivet invited a large number of guests, and Octave no longer found occasion to visit Paris so often, for Mme d'Aumale came to stay at Andilly. Seven or eight highly fashionable women arrived at the same time, most of them outstanding for their brilliance of wit or for the influence they had gained in society. But their charm only added to the triumph of the bewitching Comtesse; her mere presence in a drawing-room put years on her rivals.

Octave was too clever not to sense this, and Armance's moments of reverie became more frequent. "Whom have I to complain of?" she asked herself. "Nobody, Octave least of all. Haven't I told him I prefer another man? And he has too proud a character to be satisfied with second place in a heart. He is becoming attached to Mme d'Aumale; she's a brilliant beauty and the talk of society, and as for myself, I'm not even pretty. Whatever I can tell Octave is of very faint interest; I'm sure I often bore him, or else I interest him as a sister would. Mme d'Aumale's life is gay and unusual; nothing ever languishes in the places where she happens to be, and I think I should often be bored in my aunt's salon if I were to listen to what is said there." Armance wept, but her noble spirit did not stoop so low as to feel hatred for Mme d'Aumale. She observed every one of the actions of that charming woman with a profound attention which very often led her momentarily into lively admiration. But each act of admiration was a dagger-thrust in her heart. Her tranquil happiness disappeared, and Armance became a prey to every anguish of the passions. Mme d'Aumale's presence began to upset her more than that of Octave himself. The torments of jealousy are particularly frightful when they rend those hearts who both by inclination and by position are equally forbidden recourse to slightly indiscreet ways of pleasing.

CHAPTER XVI

Let Rome in Tyber melt! and the wide arch
Of the rang'd empire fall! Here is my space;
Kingdoms are clay: our dungy earth alike
Feeds beast as man: the nobleness of life
Is to love thus.   *Antony and Cleopatra, Act I*

ONE EVENING, after a day of stifling heat, they were
strolling leisurely in the pretty chestnut groves that
crown the heights of Andilly. By day these woods are
sometimes spoilt by the presence of the inquisitive. On that
lovely night, under the calm light of a beautiful summer moon,
these secluded hills were as though enchanted. A gentle breeze
played through the trees, adding the last touch of charm to the
delicious evening. I know not what caprice moved Mme
d'Aumale that evening, but she wished to have Octave beside
her all the time; she reminded him complacently and without
the least consideration for the men who surrounded her that it
had been in these woods that she had first seen him: "You
were disguised as a magician, and never was a first encounter
more prophetic," she added, "for you have never bored me, and
there is no other man of whom I can say as much."

Armance, who was walking with them, could not prevent
herself from finding these reminiscences very touching. Nothing could be more attractive than this brilliant Comtesse,
usually so gay, condescending to discuss in a serious voice
matters of vital interest and the ways by which to reach happiness. Octave drew apart from Mme d'Aumale's group and
soon, finding himself with Armance a few steps away from the

108

rest of the strollers, he began to relate, in the greatest detail, all that part of his life story with which Mme d'Aumale was involved. "I sought this brilliant liaison," he said, "in order not to shock Mme de Bonnivet's prudence, for had I not taken this precaution she might well have finished by ousting me from her circle of intimates." So tender a thing was said without speaking of love.

When Armance could hope that her voice would no longer betray the extreme confusion into which this statement had thrown her, she ventured: "I believe all you have told me, my dear cousin; I believe it as I should; I'm sure it's all gospel truth. None the less I notice that you have never before waited until one of your projects was so far advanced, without telling me about it."

"As to that, I have an answer all ready. Mlle Méry de Tersan and you have occasionally taken the liberty of laughing at my successes; two months ago, for instance, you almost accused me of being conceited. Even then I might perfectly well have confided to you the deliberate feelings I have for Mme d'Aumale; but it was necessary that I should be well treated by her before your eyes. Before I had been successful, your wicked wit would have seized the opportunity to make fun of my little plans. Today only Mlle de Tersan's presence is lacking to make my happiness complete."

The deep and almost tender tones in which Octave spoke these vain words betokened how utterly impossible it was that he should love the somewhat daring graces of the pretty woman about whom he was speaking, and how passionately he was devoted to the friend in whom he was confiding, so that she had not the courage to resist the happiness of finding herself so dear to him. She leaned upon Octave's arm and listened to him as if rapt in ecstasy. All that her prudence could counsel her was not to speak; the tone of her voice would have revealed to her cousin all the passion he had inspired. The light rustle of the leaves in the evening breeze seemed to lend

109

new charm to their silence.

Octave looked into Armance's large eyes gazing at his. Suddenly they became aware of a certain sound which for some time had been reaching their ears without attracting their attention. Mme d'Aumale, surprised by Octave's absence, and realizing she missed him, was calling him at the top of her voice. "Someone's calling you," said Armance, and the broken tones in which she spoke these simple words would have told anyone but Octave that he was beloved. But so surprised was he by what was happening in his heart, so disturbed by Armance's beautiful arm, almost invisibly veiled in a light gauze, which he held to his breast, that he had no attention to spare for anything. He was beside himself, tasting the pleasures of the happiest love, and almost admitting it to himself. He looked at Armance's hat, which was charming; he looked into her eyes. Never had Octave found himself placed in a position so fatal to his vows against love. He had thought he was joking as usual with Armance, and the joke had suddenly taken a turn both serious and unforeseen. He felt himself carried away, he was no longer thinking, he was utterly happy. It was one of those swift instants that chance sometimes grants, in compensation for so many sorrows, to souls capable of vigorous feeling. Life rushes in upon their hearts, love blots out the memory of all that is not divine as love is, and one lives more in a moment or two than during long measures of time.

Mme d'Aumale's voice could still be heard from time to time, calling "Octave!"; and the sound of this voice was stripping the last rags of prudence from poor Armance. Octave felt that he ought to release the beautiful arm which he was holding quite tightly to his breast; he ought to detach himself from Armance; he was within an ace, as he left her, of daring to take her hand and press it to his lips. Armance, had he permitted himself this sign of love, was in such a turmoil at that moment that she would have showed and perhaps confessed all she felt for him.

110

They rejoined the other strollers. Octave walked a little ahead. No sooner did Mme d'Aumale catch sight of him than she said a little sulkily, in such a way that Armance could not hear her : "I'm surprised to see you again so soon; how ever did you manage to leave Armance for me? You're in love with this beautiful cousin; don't trouble to deny it, I know what I'm talking about."

Octave had not yet recovered from the intoxication which had just taken possession of him; he was still aware of Armance's beautiful arm pressed against his heart. Mme d'Aumale's remark struck him like a thunderbolt, and left him stunned.

The frivolous voice seemed to him like the judgment of destiny from on high. He thought it sounded quite extraordinary. This unexpected remark, in revealing to Octave how matters really stood with his heart, hurled him from the zenith of happiness into misery that was terrible and without hope.

CHAPTER XVII

What is a man,
If his chief good, and market of his time,
Be but to sleep, and feed: a beast, no more.
... Rightly to be great
Is, not to stir without great argument;
But greatly to find quarrel in a straw,
When honour's at the stake.

Hamlet, Act IV

THEN HE had been weak enough to violate the oaths he had sworn himself so many times! A moment had overthrown his whole life's work. He had just lost all his right to self-esteem. Henceforth the world was shut to him : he had not enough virtue to live in it. There was nothing left for him but solitude, and to dwell in the midst of a desert. Such an access of sorrow and its unforeseen onset might have thrown the most resolute soul into a little confusion. Fortunately Octave realised at once that if he did not answer Mme d'Aumale quickly and with the greatest calm, Armance's reputation might suffer. He spent all his time with her, and Mme d'Aumale's remark had been seized upon by two or three persons who detested him as well as Armance.

"I, in love!" he exclaimed to Mme d'Aumale. "Alas, that's an advantage which heaven has apparently denied me; I have never felt this more keenly nor regretted it more actively. Every day, and less often than I should choose, I see the most entrancing woman in Paris; to please her is doubtless the finest ambition that a young man of my age can possess. Doubtless she would have spurned my homage; but the fact is that I have never felt within myself the degree of madness which would have made me worthy to offer it. In her presence I have never been swayed from perfect composure. After such a proof of my unsociability and insensitiveness, I despair of ever getting out of my depth with any woman."

Octave had never before spoken in such a way. This almost parliamentary explanation was skilfully prolonged and avidly listened to. There were two or three very attractive men present who often thought to see a fortunate rival in Octave. The latter was lucky enough to think of some piquant remarks. He spoke a good deal, continued to spread alarm among the amours-propres, and at length had reason to hope that everyone had forgotten about the all too true remark which Mme d'Aumale had let slip.

She had said it in a heartfelt way; Octave thought he ought to turn her attention strongly upon herself. Having proved that he could not love, for the first time in his life he indulged, with Mme d'Aumale, in half-hints bordering on tenderness; at which she was amazed.

By the end of the evening Octave felt so sure he had disarmed all suspicion, that he began to find time to think of himself. He shrank from the moment when they would disperse, and he would be free to look his misfortune in the face. He began to count the hours chimed by the château clock; midnight had long ago struck, but the night was so beautiful that to prolong it was a pleasure. One o'clock struck, and Mme d'Aumale bid her friends goodnight.

Octave had one more moment of respite. He had to go and find his mother's manservant to tell him he would be spending the night in Paris. This duty done, he plunged back into the wood, and here words fail me to give any idea of the sorrow which took possession of the unfortunate wretch. "I am in love," he muttered in a stifled tone; "I—in love! Ye Gods!"

And with his heart tautened, his throat constricted, his eyes staring and raised to the sky, he stayed motionless as though petrified with horror; a few moments later he was walking with great headlong strides. Unable to hold himself up, he dropped on to the trunk of an old tree which lay across the path, and at that moment he seemed to see even more clearly the whole extent of his misfortune.

"I had nothing to my credit except my self-esteem," he told himself; "now I've lost it." The admission of his love, which he made quite unmistakably and without finding any means of denial, was followed by convulsions of rage and inarticulate cries of fury. Mental anguish can go no further.

One idea, the usual recourse of those both unfortunate and courageous, occurred to him almost at once; but he said to himself : "If I take my life, Armance will be compromised; the whole of society will spend a week inquisitively prying into the minutest details of this evening, and every one of those gentlemen who were present will feel sanctioned to tell a different tale."

Nothing selfish, nothing of what belongs to the interests of the common run, was present in this noble spirit to combat the onslaughts of the frightful anguish which ravaged him. This absence of all commonness which might be capable of creating a diversion at such moments, is one of the tribulations that heaven seems to take pleasure in inflicting upon great souls.

The hours slipped by without diminishing Octave's despair. Motionless sometimes for several minutes on end, he knew the dreadful anguish which is the supreme torment of the greatest criminals : he despised himself absolutely.

He could not weep. The shame he thought he so fully deserved prevented him from feeling pity for himself, and arrested his tears. "Ah !" he cried in one of these cruel moments, "if only I could put an end to it all !" and he allowed himself to linger in imagination upon the idea of ceasing to feel. How joyfully he would have put himself to death as a punishment for his weak-

114

ness, and as though to offer himself honourable amends! "Yes," he told himself, "my heart deserves contempt because it has committed an act which I had forbidden myself on pain of death; and my brain is, if possible, even more contemptible than my heart. I failed to see something evident: I love Armance, and have loved her since I submitted to listen to Mme de Bonnivet's lectures on German philosophy.

"I had the folly to believe myself a philosopher. In my stupid presumptuousness I considered myself infinitely superior to Mme de Bonnivet's vain arguments, and I couldn't see in my heart what the feeblest woman would have read plain in hers: a powerful, obvious passion, and one which for a long time has been destroying all the interest I used to take in life.

"Anything which does not speak to me of Armance is as nothing to me. I was for ever assessing myself, yet I never saw these things! Oh, how contemptible I am!"

The voice of duty, which was beginning to make itself heard, was urging Octave to flee from Mlle de Zohiloff immediately; but away from her he could visualize no action which was worth living for. Nothing seemed of sufficient value to inspire him with the slightest interest. Everything seemed equally insipid, the most noble act just as the most vulgarly utilitarian: marching off to the help of Greece, and going to get killed beside Fabvier, just as conducting obscure experiments in farming in the wilds of some département.

His imagination ran swiftly over the whole gamut of possible actions, only to fall back more agonisedly into the very deepest despair, utterly without hope, most worthy of its name; ah! how welcome death would have been in those moments!

Octave spoke out loud to himself, saying things that were mad and in bad taste, and he observed their madness and bad taste with curiosity. "What's the good of deluding myself any more," he cried suddenly in the middle of describing to himself certain agricultural experiments to be carried out among the peasants of Brazil. "What's the good of being cowardly enough to go on deluding myself? As a crowning sorrow I can tell myself that Armance is in love with me, and my duties are all the more exacting because of it. Why; if Armance were betrothed, would the man to whom she had promised her hand have passively allowed her to spend all her time entirely with me? And her joy, apparently so calm, but so deep and sincere, when I told her last night about my plan of behaviour with Mme d'Aumale—what can explain that? Isn't that a proof clearer than daylight? And yet I could deceive myself. But then I must have been guilty of hypocrisy to myself, mustn't I? But then I must have followed in the footsteps of the vilest scoundrels? Think of it! Last night at ten o'clock I failed to perceive something which a few hours later seems utterly self-evident! Oh, how weak and contemptible I am!

"With all the arrogant pride of a child, in all my life I have never once risen to act like a man; and not only have I been the author of my own misfortune, but I have dragged down into the abyss the one being whom I hold dearest in the whole world. Oh ye gods! What would a man have to do to be viler than I?" This moment verged upon delirium. Octave's head was as though disintegrated by a burning heat. At every step taken by his intellect, he discovered a new degree of misfortune, a new reason to despise himself.

That instinct towards comfort which is always present in man, even at the cruellest moments—even at the foot of the scaffold—caused Octave to attempt, as it were, to stop himself thinking. He pressed his two hands tightly against his head, as though by physical efforts he could cease to think.

Gradually he became indifferent to everything, except the memory of Armance from whom he must escape for ever, and never see her again on any account. Even filial love, so deeply impressed there, had disappeared from his soul.

He had but two ideas now, to leave Armance and never to allow himself to see her again; in this way to withstand life for a year or two, until she should be married or until society had forgotten about him. After which, since no one would have any further thought for him, he would be free to make an end. This was the last sentiment felt by his soul, worn out with suffering. Octave leant against a tree and dropped down in a faint.

When he came back to his senses, he felt that he was extraordinarily cold. He opened his eyes. Day was breaking. He found himself being tended by a peasant who was trying to bring him round by fetching water in his hat from a nearby spring, and pouring it over him. Octave was confused for a moment; his thoughts were not at all clear; he observed that he was lying on the bank of a ditch, in the middle of a clearing, in a wood; he could see large roundish patches of mist floating swiftly past him. He did not recognize the place where he was.

Suddenly all his misfortunes crowded in upon his thoughts. One does not die of anguish, or he would have died at that moment. He uttered one or two cries which alarmed the peasant. The fright of the man recalled Octave to his sense of duty. It was necessary that this peasant should hold his tongue. Octave took out his purse to offer him some money; he told the man, who seemed to feel pity for his condition, that he was in the wood at this hour because of an imprudent wager, and that it was most important to him that no one should know that the coldness of the night had made him unwell.

The peasant appeared not to understand.

"If people knew I had fainted," said Octave, "they would laugh at me."

"Ah, I understand," said the peasant; "trust me, I shan't breathe a word; it won't be said that I made you lose your wager. But it's lucky for you I was passing, for upon my soul you looked as if you were dead."

Octave, instead of heeding him, was looking at his purse. Here was a new pain; it was a present from Armance; he took pleasure in feeling under his fingertips each of the little steel beads sewn on to the dark material.

As soon as the peasant had left him, Octave broke off a

young chestnut stem, with which he made a hole in the ground; he went so far as to impress a kiss upon the purse, the present from Armance, and he buried it at the exact spot where he had fainted. "This," he said to himself, "is my first virtuous act. Farewell, farewell for life, dearest Armance! Heaven can bear witness whether I have loved you!"

CHAPTER XVIII

Upon her alabaster bosom she wears a brilliant
cross, where the child of Jacob would press his
lips with respect, and the infidel adore.

Schiller

URGED BY some instinct he hastened towards the château.
He felt confusedly that reasoning with himself was the
greatest of all evils; but he had seen where his duty lay,
and relied upon finding within himself the courage necessary
to accomplish whatever actions might be required. He justified
his return to the château—prompted by a horror of remaining
alone—by the notion that some servant or other could well
arrive from Paris and say that he had not been seen in the Rue
Saint-Dominique, and this might expose his folly to discovery
and make his mother anxious.

Octave was quite far from the château. "Ah!" he thought,
as he crossed through the wood to return, "only yesterday there
were some children hunting here; if some clumsy child shooting
at a bird from behind a hedge could kill me, then I should have
nothing to reproach myself with. Lord, how wonderful it would
be to get a bullet in this burning head of mine! How I should
thank him before I died—if I had time!"

It will be seen that Octave's behaviour was a little tinged
with madness that morning. The romantic hope of being shot
by a child caused him to slacken his pace, and his soul, because
of a tiny weakness, which he half recognized, refused to consider the legitimacy of this action. At length he re-entered the

château by the little garden gate, and the first person he saw was Armance. He stopped dead, and his blood froze; he had not thought to meet her so soon. No sooner did she catch sight of him in the distance than Armance ran towards him smiling; she was as light and graceful as a bird; he had never seen her look so pretty; she was thinking of what he had told her the previous evening about his affair with Mme d'Aumale.

"So I'm seeing her for the last time," thought Octave, and looked at her eagerly. Armance's big straw hat, her noble figure, the heavy curls loosely about her cheeks, which were in such charming contrast with those glances of hers, at once so penetrating and so gentle : all these he sought to engrave upon his soul. But her laughing looks very quickly lost their air of happiness as Armance drew nearer. It seemed to her that there was something sinister in Octave's behaviour. She noticed that his clothes were soaking wet.

She asked him in a voice unsteady with emotion : "What's the matter with you, cousin ?" As she spoke these simple words, she could hardly restrain her tears, so clearly did she perceive a strange expression on his face.

"Mademoiselle," he replied icily, "you will allow me to remain unappreciative of an interest which dogs me in such a way as to deprive me of all freedom. It's perfectly true; I have just arrived from Paris and my clothes are damp. If these explanations do not satisfy curiosity, I shall give you more detailed ones. . . ." Here Octave's cruelty came to a halt despite himself.

Armance, who had turned mortally pale, seemed to be making vain efforts to move away; she was visibly staggering and on the point of falling. He approached her to offer his arm; Armance looked at him with languishing eyes, that seemed besides robbed of all power to reflect ideas.

Octave took her hand quite abruptly, tucked it under his arm, and walked off towards the château. But he felt that he too was without strength; on the verge of falling himself, he

120

nevertheless summoned up the courage to tell her: "I am going away—I have to go on a long journey to America; I shall write; I count on you to solace my mother; tell her I shall certainly come back. As for yourself, Mademoiselle, it has been claimed that I am in love with you; I myself am very far from making so bold a claim. Besides, the longstanding friendship which unites us should have been enough, as I see it, to thwart the birth of love. We know each other too well to entertain for one another the kind of feeling which always presupposes a measure of illusion."

At that moment Armance found that she could walk no more; she raised her downcast eyes and looked at Octave; her lips, bloodless and trembling, seemed to be trying to utter a few words. She tried to support herself upon the tub of an orange-tree, but had not the strength to hold up; she slipped and fell beside the tree, quite unconscious.

Without making a move to help her, Octave stood still and watched her; she was in a deep swoon, her beautiful eyes were half open, and the contours of her charming mouth had retained an expression of deep sorrow. All the rare perfection of that delicate body was betrayed by her simple morning gown. Octave noticed a little diamond cross which Armance was wearing that day for the first time.

He was weak enough to seize her hand. All his philosophy had deserted him. He saw that the tub of the orange-tree hid him from the curiosity of those in the château; he knelt down beside Armance: "Forgive me, oh my dearest angel," he said in a low voice, covering her icy hand with kisses, "never have I loved you so much!"

Armance stirred; Octave jumped up convulsively; soon Armance was able to walk, and he conducted her back to the château without daring to look at her. He was reproaching himself bitterly for the shameful weakness into which he had been swept; if Armance had perceived it, then all the cruelty of his earlier remarks was now useless. She made haste to leave him once they had entered the château.

The moment Mme de Malivert was ready to receive visitors, Octave was shown in and threw himself into her arms. "Mother dear, give me your permission to travel; it's the only course left open to me to avoid a hateful marriage, unless I am to be wanting in the respect I owe to my father." Mme de Malivert, greatly astonished, tried in vain to make her son give her a few more positive details about this alleged marriage.

"Well indeed!" she exclaimed, "neither the young lady's name nor any hint of her family—you have no information for me at all! But this is madness!" Soon Mme de Malivert felt she dared no longer use that word, for it seemed to ring too true. All she could extract from her son, who appeared determined to leave that very day, was that he would not go to America. The destination of his journey was all one to Octave, who had only been thinking of the anguish of departure.

As he was speaking to his mother and trying, in order not to frighten her, to moderate his ideas a little, a plausible reason suddenly occurred to him. "Mother dear, a man who bears the name of de Malivert and who has had the misfortune to have achieved nothing by the age of twenty ought to begin by going to the Crusades as our ancestors did. I beg you to allow me to go to Greece. If you insist I will tell my father that I am going to Naples; once there, as if by chance, I shall be drawn by curiosity towards Greece, and would it not be natural for a gentleman to see it sword in hand? This method of breaking the news of my journey will strip it of all pretentiousness. . . ."

This plan caused Mme de Malivert lively anxiety; but there was something generous about it, and it accorded with her idea of duty. After two hours of discussion, which were moments of respite for Octave, he obtained his mother's consent. Close in the arms of this loving friend, for a brief moment he knew the happiness of being able to weep. He consented to conditions he would have refused when he first entered her room. He promised her that if she wished it, twelve months from the day he disembarked in Greece he would come and spend a fortnight with her.

"But mother, my dear, to avoid the unpleasantness of reading about my journey in the newspaper, please do agree to receive me at your estate at Malivert, in Dauphiné." All was arranged as he wished it, and the conditions of this unexpected departure sealed with tears of tenderness.

On leaving his mother, Octave, having fulfilled his duty towards Armance, summoned the necessary composure to pay a visit to the Marquis. "Father," he said when he had embraced him, "allow your son to put a question to you : what was the first action of Enguerrand de Malivert, who lived in 1147, in the reign of Louis the Young ?"

The Marquis opened his bureau eagerly, and took from it a handsome roll of parchment which never left his possession : it was the genealogical tree of the family. He observed with the greatest pleasure that his son's memory had served him well. "Well, my boy," said the old man, putting his spectacles down before him, "Enguerrand de Malivert left upon a Crusade in 1147, with his king !"

"Wasn't he nineteen at that time ?" pursued Octave.

"Exactly nineteen," said the Marquis, more and more satisfied by the respect the young Vicomte was evincing for the family tree.

When Octave had allowed time for his father's feeling of content to fill out and establish itself thoroughly in the old man's soul, he said resolutely : "Father, *noblesse oblige!* I am more than twenty, and have spent enough time at my books. I come to ask your blessing and your permission to go travelling in Italy and Sicily. I shall not conceal from you—though it is to you alone that I make the admission—that from Sicily I shall be drawn to proceed to Greece; I shall make a point of taking part in a battle, and shall return to you perhaps a little more worthy of the fine name which you have handed down to me."

Although the Marquis was a very brave man, he was not

123

endowed with the soul of his ancestors in the time of Louis the Young; he was a father, and a doting father in the nineteenth century. Octave's sudden resolve left him quite at a loss for words; he would willingly have made do with a less heroic son. Nevertheless he was impressed by the austere expression of this same son, and the resolute firmness revealed by his behaviour. Strength of character had never been his speciality, and he did not dare refuse a permission which was requested in such a way as to suggest that if he refused, it could quite well be done without.

"You touch me to the heart," the old fellow said as he crossed over to his bureau; and although his son had not asked it of him he drew a note of hand for quite a large sum, upon a notary who held funds of his. "Take this," he said to Octave, "and please God it may not be the last money I give you !"

The bell rang for the midday meal. Fortunately Mme d'Aumale and Mme de Bonnivet happened to be in Paris, and the sorrowing family was not obliged to conceal its grief behind vain words.

Octave, strengthened a little by a sense of having done his duty, felt he had the courage to carry on; he had intended to leave before this meal, but now he thought it would be better to do everything exactly as usual. The servants might talk. He sat at the small dining-table, face to face with Armance.

"I'm seeing her now for the last time in my life," he told himself. Armance had the good fortune to burn herself quite painfully as she was making the tea. This mischance would have served as an excuse for her confusion, had anyone in that little room been cool-headed enough to notice it. M. de Malivert's voice was shaky; for the first time in his life he could find nothing pleasant to say. He was racking his brains to see whether there was a pretext, compatible with the fine phrase *Noblesse oblige!* so aptly quoted by his son, which might conceivably enable him to delay this departure.

CHAPTER XIX

He unworthy you say?
'Tis impossible. It would
Be more easy to die.
Deckar

OCTAVE THOUGHT he observed that Mlle de Zohiloff was looking at him now and again with a certain calm. Despite his fierce virtue, which haughtily forbade him to let his thoughts dwell upon relationships no longer existing, he could not prevent himself from thinking that this was the first time he had seen her since he had admitted to himself that he loved her; in the garden that morning he had been distracted by the necessity to act. "So this," he said to himself, "is the impression created by the sight of the woman one loves. But possibly Armance feels nothing for me but friendship. It was again presumptuous of me last night to think otherwise."

During this painful meal not a word was spoken about the subject which lay upon all their hearts. While Octave had been with his father Mme de Malivert had sent for Armance to let her know of the strange plan to go travelling. The poor girl was in need of sincerity; she could not help saying to Mme de Malivert: "Well, Mother, now you can see whether your ideas were well-founded."

These two charming women were suffering the bitterest anguish. "What ever can be the reason for his going?" repeated Mme de Malivert, "for it can't be an act of madness—you've cured him of that." It was agreed that they would speak to no one about Octave's journey, not even to Mme de Bonnivet.

It was important not to bind him to his plan, "and perhaps," said Mme de Malivert, "we may yet dare to hope. He will give up an intention so abruptly conceived."

Armance's sorrow was, if possible, rendered yet more cruel by this conversation; still faithful to the vow of eternal silence she believed she owed to the feelings which existed between herself and her cousin, she suffered the burden of her discretion. The words of Mme de Malivert, such a wise friend, who loved her so dearly, were no consolation to Armance, bearing as they did upon facts of which she knew only very imperfectly.

And yet how much she must have needed to consult a friend about the various causes which, it seemed to her, might equally have resulted in such extraordinary conduct on the part of her cousin! But nothing on earth, not even the atrocious anguish that was rending her soul, could make her forget what a woman owes to herself. She would have died of shame rather than repeat the words that the man whom she preferred had spoken to her earlier in the morning. "If I were to tell a secret of that kind," she thought to herself, "and if Octave were to find out, he would respect me no longer."

When the meal was over, Octave made haste to leave for Paris. His behaviour was abrupt, and he had given up trying to account for his actions. He was beginning to feel the whole bitterness of his plan to go away, and was afraid of the danger if he should find himself alone with Armance. If her angelic goodness had not been stung by the frightening harshness of his conduct, if she condescended to speak to him, could he trust himself not to soften as he bid goodbye for ever to this cousin who was so beautiful, so perfect?

She would see that he loved her—but it would be none the less necessary to leave afterwards, and leave in eternal remorse at having failed to do one's duty even at this supreme moment. Was not his most sacred duty towards that being whom he held dearest of all on earth, and whose peace of mind he had perhaps compromised?

126

Octave left the courtyard of the château with the feelings of a man who is going to his death, and, truth to tell, he would have been happy to find his anguish merely that of the condemned being led to execution. He had feared the loneliness of his journey, yet he was hardly suffering at all; he was surprised at this moment of respite granted him by misfortune.

He had just been subjected to a lesson in modesty too severe to allow him to attribute this peace of mind to that vain philosophy which had formerly been his pride. In this respect misfortune had made a new man of him. His strength was spent by so much effort and so many violent feelings; he could feel no more. No sooner was he down from Andilly and on to the plain than he fell into a lethargic sleep, and was surprised on arriving in Paris to find himself being driven by the servant who, when they left, had been following his cabriolet.

Armance, hidden behind a shutter in the attics of the château, had followed every detail of his departure. When Octave's cabriolet had disappeared beyond the trees, she remained motionless, saying to herself: "It's all over; he won't come back".

Towards evening, after she had wept for a long time, a question which occurred to her gave her a little distraction from her sorrow. "How is it that Octave, who is so distinguished for his polite behaviour, and whose friendship was so attentive, so loyal, perhaps even so tender," she added blushing, "yesterday evening when we were walking together—how is it that he can have taken on, in a matter of a few hours, so callous, so insulting an attitude, so alien to his whole way of being? Certainly he can't have learnt anything about me which might offend him."

Armance sought to recall all the details of her conduct, secretly wishing that she might come across some fault which could justify the queer attitude Octave had adopted with her. She could find nothing reprehensible; she was wretched at being unable to see any faults in herself, when suddenly an old idea re-awoke in her mind.

Wasn't it probable that Octave had suffered a relapse into that frenzy which had formerly driven him into a number of strange acts of violence? This recollection, although extremely painful at first, came like a ray of light. Armance was so unhappy that every argument she could find soon proved to her that this was the most likely explanation. To see Octave not as unfair, whatever his excuse might be, gave her the greatest comfort.

As for his madness, if he were mad, she but loved him the more passionately for it. "He will need all my devotion—and that devotion will never be denied him," she added, her eyes bright with tears, and her heart throbbing with generosity and courage. "Perhaps just now Octave is exaggerating the obligation of a young nobleman, who has not yet made his mark, to go to the aid of Greece. Didn't his father, a few years ago, want him to take the Cross of Malta? Several members of his family have been Knights of Malta. Perhaps as he inherits their illustriousness he feels himself obliged to fulfil the oaths they took to fight against the Turks?"

Armance recalled that Octave had said to her, the day they heard of the fall of Missolonghi: "I cannot conceive how my uncle the Commandeur can remain so handsomely unmoved, he who has taken oaths and who, before the revolution, drew the benefits of a considerable allowance. And we wish to be respected by the industrial party!"

By reason of thinking upon this consoling explanation of her cousin's behaviour, Armance told herself: "Perhaps some personal motive has become linked to this general obligation by which it is very possible that Octave's noble soul thinks itself bound?

"Perhaps the idea he once had of becoming a priest, before the successes of one section of the clergy, has caused some remark to be made about him recently. Perhaps he thinks it would be more worthy of his name to go to Greece and show

128

there that he has not degenerated from his ancestors, than to seek out some obscure encounter in Paris, whose motive would always be difficult to explain and might leave a stain on his character?

"He hasn't told me all this because that kind of thing is not mentioned to a woman. He has been afraid that his habit of confiding in me might lead him to admit it to me; hence the harshness of his words. He didn't want to be carried away into making an unsuitable admission to me. . . ."

It was thus that Armance's imagination lost its way among suppositions, comforting because they depicted Octave as innocent and generous. "It is only from excess of virtue," she said to herself, with tears in her eyes, "that such a soul can appear to be in the wrong."

129

CHAPTER XX

A fine woman! a fair woman! a sweet woman!
Nay, you must forget that.
O, the world has not a sweeter creature.
                                    Othello, Act IV

W HILE ARMANCE walked alone through a part of the Andilly woods hidden from all eyes, Octave was in Paris, busy with preparations for his departure. He felt alternately a sort of calm, astonished at itself, then moments of the most poignant despair. Shall we attempt to evoke the different kinds of anguish that distinguished each instant of his life? Will not the reader tire of these dismal details?

It seemed to him that he could hear voices speaking incessantly close to his ear, and this strange and unexpected sensation prevented him from forgetting his misfortune even for a moment.

The most irrelevant objects reminded him of Armance. His madness became such that he could not see an A or a Z at the head of a placard or on the signboard of a shop without being violently swept into thoughts of the Armance de Zohiloff whom he had sworn to forget. The thought of her clung to him like a devouring flame, and held all the attractiveness of novelty, all the interest that he would have accorded it had the idea of his cousin not entered his mind for ages.

Everything conspired against him; he was helping his servant, the good Voreppe, to pack his pistols; the fellow's chatter diverted him a little, delighted as the man was to be going away along with his master, and to be in charge of all the arrangements. All at once he noticed these words engraved in abbreviated form on the stock of one of the pistols : *Armance tries to fire this weapon, September 3rd, 182*.*

He took up a map of Greece; as he unfolded it he let fall one of those pins bearing a little red flag with which Armance used to mark the position of the Turks at the time of the siege of Missolonghi.

The map of Greece slipped from his hands. He stayed motionless with despair. "So it is forbidden that I should forget!" he cried, with his eyes upraised. In vain he sought to take himself firmly in hand. Everything which surrounded him bore the marks of Armance's memory. The initials of that dear name were written everywhere, followed by some date of interest.

Octave wandered aimlessly about his room; he gave orders only to countermand them a second later. "Oh, I don't know what I want!" he told himself, at the pitch of his anguish. "Heavens, how can one suffer more?"

He found no relief, whatever position he tried. He made the most extraordinary gestures. If for a split second he could achieve a tinge of surprise and of physical pain, it distracted him from the thought of Armance. Every time his spirit recalled the image of Armance he tried to cause himself quite acute physical pain. Of all the shifts he devised this was the least useless.

At other moments he said to himself : "So I am never to see her again! This is the culminating sorrow of them all. It's a steely weapon whose point I must blunt by dint of thrusting it into my heart."

He sent his servant out to buy a few of the necessities for the journey; he felt a need to be rid of the man's presence; he wanted for a few moments to surrender himself to his frightful sorrow. Constraint seemed to envenom it still more.

Not five minutes after the servant had left the room he felt

131

that he would have found relief in being able to talk to him; suffering in solitude had become the worst of torments. "And not to be able to kill oneself!" he cried. He went over to the window to try and see something which might engage his attention for a moment.

Evening came; drink was no help to him. He had hoped it might give him a little sleep; it did nothing but drive him mad.

Terrified by the ideas which entered his mind and which might make him the laughing-stock of the family and indirectly compromise Armance, he locked himself in, exclaiming: "It would be better if I allowed myself to make an end."

Night was well advanced; motionless on the balcony outside his window, he looked at the sky. The least sound caught his notice; but one by one all sounds ceased. This utter silence, leaving him wholly to himself, seemed to him to add yet more horror to his position. No sooner did extreme weariness obtain him a second of near-rest, than the confused murmur of human speech which he seemed to hear close to his ear awoke him with a start.

The next morning, when they came to call him, the moral torment goading him to action was so excruciating that he felt he wanted to fling his arms round the neck of the barber who was cutting his hair, and tell him how much he was to be pitied. The wretch under the torture of the surgeon's lancet thinks to relieve his pain with a savage cry.

At the most bearable moments Octave felt the need to carry on a conversation with his manservant. The most childish trivialities seemed to absorb his entire attention, and he applied himself to them with remarkable care.

His misfortune had left him with an excessive modesty. Each time he recalled to mind one of those little disagreements that one meets in society, he was invariably surprised at the not very courteous energy he had expended; it seemed to him that his antagonist had been completely right and he himself completely wrong.

The picture of each one of the misfortunes he had encountered in his life displayed itself to him with painful intensity; and because he was never to see Armance again the recollection of that host of little ills which one of her glances would have swept from his mind, returned more bitterly than ever. He who had so hated tedious visits now longed for them. A stupid fool who called on him was his benefactor for an hour.

He had a formal letter to write to a distant relation; she was later tempted to see in it a declaration of love, so sincerely and profoundly did he speak of himself, and so clear was it that the author was in need of pity.

In the midst of these painful alternatives, Octave had reached the evening of the second day since he had left Armance; he had been to see his saddler, and was just coming away. All his preparations were at last to be completed during that night, and from the following morning he would be ready to leave.

Should he return to Andilly? That was the question he was arguing with himself. He could see with horror that he no longer loved his mother, for she figured not at all in the reasons he advanced for revisiting Andilly. He shrank from seeing Mlle de Zohiloff, the more so in that at times he kept asking himself: "But isn't my whole behaviour a sham?"

He dared not reply: "Yes", but at that point the party of temptation would suggest: "Is it not a sacred duty to see my poor mother again, as I promised her I should?" "No, wretch!" would cry conscience; "that reply is but a trick—you no longer love your mother."

At this moment of anguish his eyes lingered mechanically upon a playbill, on which he read the word *Otello*, printed in very large letters. This word reminded him of the existence of Mme d'Aumale. "Perhaps she will have come to Paris for *Otello*; in that case it's my duty to speak to her once more. I must make her see this sudden journey of mine as the idea of a man who is bored. I have concealed the plan from my friends for a long time; but for several months my departure has been delayed only by money difficulties of a sort that one can't speak of to rich friends."

CHAPTER XXI

Durate, et vosmet rebus servate secundis.
Virgil

O CTAVE ENTERED the Théâtre Italien; and there indeed was Mme d'Aumale; with her in her box was a certain Marquis de Crêveroche; he was one of the most importunate of the fops who beset that attractive woman, but either with less wits or more complacency than the others, he thought himself elect. No sooner did Octave show his face than Mme d'Aumale had eyes for no one else, and the Marquis de Crêveroche, beside himself with resentment, left without their even noticing his departure.

Octave settled himself against the rail of the box and from force of habit—for on that day he was far from seeking affectation of any kind—he began talking to Mme d'Aumale in a voice which sometimes drowned those of the actors. We must confess that he somewhat overstepped the tolerated limits of impertinence, and had the pit of the Théâtre Italien been made up like those of other playhouses, he would have experienced the diversion of a public scene.

In the middle of the second act of *Otello*, the little messenger who sells the opera libretti, and calls them in a nasal voice, came and delivered him the following note:

"Sir,
I am naturally quite contemptuous of all affectations; one sees so many in society that I take notice of them only when

they annoy me. You annoy me by the din you are creating with the little d'Aumale girl. Kindly be silent.

I have the honour to be, etc.,

The Marquis de Crêveroche.

Rue de Verneuil, n° 54."

Octave was profoundly astonished by this note, which recalled him to all the vulgar cares of life; at first he was like a man who has been hoisted out of hell for an instant. His first idea was to affect the joy which soon pervaded his spirits. It occurred to him that M. de Crêveroche's opera-glass was probably trained upon Mme d'Aumale's box, and that it would be a score to his rival if she were to appear to be enjoying herself any less after his note.

This word *rival* which he used to himself made him burst out laughing; he had an odd look in his eye. "What's the matter with you?" asked Mme d'Aumale. "I'm thinking of my rivals. Can there be on this earth another man who claims to please you as much as I do?" So handsome a remark was worth more to the young Comtesse than the most passionate strains of the sublime Pasta.

Very late that night, after he had taken home Mme d'Aumale, who wished to have supper, Octave, left to himself, was calm and cheerful. What a difference from the state he had been in since the night spent in the forest!

It was none too simple for him to lay hands on a second. His manner was so discouragingly aloof, and he had so few friends, that he was extremely afraid of being indiscreet in asking one of his sportive companions to accompany him to M. de Crêveroche's. At last he bethought him of a certain M. Dolier, an officer on half pay, whom he saw very seldom, but who was related to him.

At three in the morning he sent a note in to M. Dolier's porter; at half past five he was there in person, and shortly afterwards the two gentlemen called upon M. de Crêveroche, who received them with a politeness which, although somewhat mannered, was beyond question perfectly correct. "I was awaiting you, gentlemen," he told them airily; "I have been entertaining the hope that you would be good enough to do me the honour of taking tea with my friend M. de Meylan, whom I have the honour to present, and myself."

They had some tea. As he rose from the table, M. de Crêveroche named the Bois de Meudon.

"That fellow's affected politeness is beginning to put me out of temper, for my part," said the officer of the old army as he climbed back into Octave's cabriolet. "Let me have the reins; don't spoil your hand. How long is it since you saw the inside of a fencing-school?"

"Three or four years," said Octave. "As far back as I can remember."

"When did you last fire a pistol?"

"Perhaps six months ago, but I never thought of fighting with a pistol."

"The devil take it," exclaimed M. Dolier, "six months! That's most annoying. Here, hold out your arm. You're shaking like a leaf."

"It's an affliction I have always suffered," said Octave.

M. Dolier, much dissatisfied, said no more. The hour of silence they spent on the way from Paris to Meudon was sweeter to Octave than any moment he had passed since his misfortune. He had in no way sought out this quarrel. He intended to defend himself stoutly; but after all, if he were killed, he would have nothing to reproach himself with. Considering the state his affairs were in, death would bring him the greatest happiness.

They reached a remote corner of the Bois de Meudon, but M. de Crêveroche, more affected and dandified than ever, made ridiculous objections to two or three places. M. Dolier could hardly contain himself, and Octave found it difficult to restrain him. "At least let me tackle his second," said M. Dolier. "I

137

want to make it clear to him what I think of the pair of them."

"Put those ideas off until tomorrow," replied Octave severely; "please bear in mind that today you have been good enough to promise me your help."

M. de Crêveroche's second suggested pistols before mentioning swords. Octave found this in poor taste and signed to M. Dolier who accepted at once. At last they were ready to fire; M. de Crêveroche, a very skilful marksman, had the first shot; Octave was hit in the thigh, and began to bleed copiously. "I have the right to fire," he said coldly; and M. de Crêveroche received a graze on the leg. "Bind up my thigh with my handkerchief and your own," said Octave to his servant; "you've got to stop the bleeding for a minute or two." "What do you propose to do, then?" asked M. Dolier. "To carry on," answered Octave. "I don't feel weak at all; I've as much strength as when I arrived here; I should finish off any other kind of business, so why not bring this one to a conclusion?" "But it seems to me more than concluded already," said M. Dolier. "And what about your anger ten minutes ago; what has happened to that?" "The man hasn't tried to insult us in any way," replied M. Dolier; "he's simply a fool."

The seconds, after consultation, declared themselves firmly against any resumption of fire. Octave had perceived that M. de Crêveroche's second was an inferior person, perhaps having got on in society by his deeds of valour, but fundamentally in a state of constant adoration before the Marquis; he spoke a few pointed words to him. M. de Meylan was reduced to silence by a stern word from his friend, and Octave's second could no longer decently make further comment. Even as he was speaking Octave felt perhaps happier than he had ever been in his life before. I know not what vague and criminal hope he founded upon his wound, which was to keep him for a few days at his mother's, and in consequence not very far from Armance. At last, after a quarter of an hour, M. de Crêveroche, flushed with anger, and Octave, the happiest man

138

alive, obtained that the pistols should be reloaded.

M. de Crêveroche, infuriated by the fear of being unable to dance for several weeks because of the scratch on his leg, vainly suggested they should fire point-blank; the seconds threatened to abandon them there with their servants, and to take away the pistols, if they moved so much as a step nearer to each other. Chance again favoured M. de Crêveroche; he took a long aim, and wounded Octave severely in the right arm. "Sir," Octave shouted at him, "you must await my shot; permit me to have my arm bandaged." When this operation had been swiftly carried out, and Octave's servant, an old soldier, had soaked the handkerchief in brandy, which caused it to hold very firmly, Octave said to M. Dolier: "I feel quite strong enough." He fired, M. de Crêveroche fell, and died two minutes later.

Octave, supported by his servant, returned to his cabriolet and entered it without a word. M. Dolier could not help feeling pity for the handsome young man who lay dying, and whose limbs they could see stiffening only a few paces away. "It's merely one fop the less," Octave said coldly.

Twenty minutes later, although the cabriolet was moving only at a walk, Octave turned to M. Dolier and said: "my arm's hurting me; this handkerchief is too tight;" then all at once he fainted. He did not recover consciousness until an hour later, in the cottage of a gardener, a good-natured fellow whom M. Dolier had begun by paying handsomely on entering his home.

"My dear cousin," said Octave, "you know how unwell my mother is; leave me here and go to the Rue Saint-Dominique; if you don't find my mother in Paris, please do me the great favour of going on to Andilly; tell her as tactfully as you possibly can that I've had a fall from a horse and broken a bone in my right arm. Don't mention either duels or bullets. I have reason to hope that certain circumstances of which I will tell you later may prevent my mother from being cast into despair by the news of this minor injury; say nothing of duels except to the police if you have to, and send me a surgeon. If you go as far as the château at Andilly, which is five minutes from the village, ask to see Mlle Armance de Zohiloff—she will prepare my mother for the story you have to tell her."

To have spoken Armance's name caused an upheaval in Octave's situation. So he dared, then, to pronounce that name, something he had so sternly forbidden himself! Maybe he would not be leaving her for a month! He knew an instant of complete bliss.

During the duel the idea of Armance had frequently been close to Octave's mind, but he had strictly dismissed it. After he had said her name, he dared for a moment to think about her; just afterwards he felt very weak. "Ah, if I were about to die," he said to himself with joy, and allowed his mind to dwell upon Armance as it had done before the fatal discovery that he loved her. Octave noticed that the peasants who surrounded him looked exceedingly alarmed; the signs of their anxiety lessened his remorse at having allowed himself to think of his cousin. "If my wounds go badly," he thought, "it will be permissible to write to her. I've been very cruel to her."

The idea of writing to Armance, once it had appeared, took complete possession of Octave's wits. "If I feel better," he told himself at last, to lull his self-reproach, "I can always burn my letter." Octave was in a good deal of pain, and was now suffering from a violent headache; "I might die at any moment," he said to himself cheerfully, doing his best to recall some ideas of anatomy. "Oh, surely I must be allowed to write!"

At length he succumbed to the weakness of asking for quill, paper and ink. A sheet of coarse school paper and a bad quill were easily procured, but there was no ink in the house. Dare we admit it? Octave was so childish as to write with the blood which was still seeping a little through the binding of his right arm. He wrote with his left hand, and with less difficulty than he had expected:

"My dear cousin,

I have just received two injuries each of which may keep me at home for a fortnight. As, after my mother, you are the being for whom in all the world I have the greatest reverence, I am writing you these lines to acquaint you with the above fact. If I were running any risk I should tell you so. You have made me accustomed to take your tender friendship for granted; please would you be kind enough to go and stay beside my mother as if by chance; M. Dolier is going to tell her simply about a fall from a horse and a fractured right arm. Did you know, my dear Armance, that we have two bones in that part of the arm which is joined to the hand? It is one of these bones which is broken. Of all the injuries that keep people at home for a month, this is the simplest I can imagine. I do not know whether propriety will allow that you should come and see me during my illness; I fear not. I have a fancy to commit an indiscretion : because of my narrow staircase they will perhaps suggest that my bed should be placed in the drawing-room through which one has to pass to reach my mother's room, and I shall accept. I beg you to burn my letter without a moment's delay. . . . I have just fainted; it is the natural and not at all dangerous consequence of haemorrhage—you see I am already using learned words. You were my last thought as I lost consciousness, and my first as I came to my senses. If you think it decent, come to Paris before my mother; the moving of an injured man, even when it is a mere matter of a sprained ankle, always has something sinister about it which she must be spared. One of your misfortunes, dear Armance, is to have your parents no longer; if I should by chance die—against all likelihood—you will be bereft of him who loved you better than a father loves his daughter.

141

May God grant you the happiness you deserve, which is to say a very, very great deal.

Octave

P.S. Forgive certain harsh words, which were necessary at the time."

The idea of death having occurred to Octave, he sent for a second sheet of paper, in the middle of which he wrote :

> "I bequeath the ownership of all I possess at this moment to Mlle Armance de Zohiloff my cousin, in humble token of my gratitude for the care I am sure she will bestow upon my mother when I am no more.
>
> As witness my hand at Clamart, the.........182*.
>
> OCTAVE DE MALIVERT

And he made two witnesses sign it, the quality of the ink affording him some misgivings as to the validity of such an instrument.

CHAPTER XXII

To the dull plodding man whose vulgar
soul is awake only to the gross and
paltry interests of everyday life, the
spectacle of a noble being plunged in
misfortune by the resistless force of
passion, serves only as an object of
scorn and ridicule.   *Deckar*

A s the witnesses were completing their signature, he
fainted again; the peasants, in a state of great anxiety,
had gone to fetch their curé. At last two surgeons
arrived from Paris and pronounced Octave's condition to be
very serious. These two gentlemen were impressed by the inconvenience they would suffer were they to travel every day
to Clamart, and decided that the invalid should be moved to
Paris.

Octave had despatched his letter to Armance by the hand
of a willing young peasant who took a horse from the stage-
post and promised he would reach the château of Andilly within two hours. The letter arrived before M. Dolier, who had
stayed some time in Paris to find surgeons. The young peasant
easily managed to have himself taken in to see Mlle de Zohiloff
without creating any stir in the household. She read the letter.
She could barely summon the strength to ask a few questions.
All her courage had deserted her.

At the time the fatal news reached her she was in that mood
of discouragement which follows great sacrifices that are dic-

tated by duty, but that have resulted in nothing but a state of motionless calm. She was trying to grow accustomed to the thought of never seeing Octave again, but the idea of his death had never occurred to her. This last blow of fortune's caught her unawares.

As she listened to the exceedingly alarming details given by the young peasant she was choked by sobs, and Mme de Bonnivet and Mme de Malivert were in the next room! Armance shuddered at the thought of being overheard by them, and of their seeing her in such a state. The sight would have killed Mme de Malivert, and later Mme de Bonnivet would have turned it into a tragic and moving anecdote thoroughly unpleasant for the heroine.

Mlle de Zohiloff could not in any circumstances allow an unhappy mother to see that letter written in the blood of her son. She seized upon the idea of making her way to Paris and taking a lady's-maid with her. This woman emboldened her to take the young peasant with her in the carriage. I shall say nothing of the sad details which were related to her during this journey. They arrived at the Rue Saint-Dominique.

She shuddered as she saw in the distance the house in one of whose rooms Octave was perhaps breathing his last. It was discovered that he had not yet arrived; Armance had no further doubts—she believed him dead in the Clamart peasant's cottage. Her despair prevented her from giving the simplest orders; at length she managed to say that a bed must be made up in the drawing-room. The astonished servants obeyed her uncomprehendingly.

Armance had sent for a carriage, and had no thought but to find an excuse which would allow her to go to Clamart. It seemed to her that everything must give place to the obligation to help Octave in his last moments if he were still alive. "What is society or its vain judgments to me?" she asked herself. "I took account of it only for him; and besides, if opinion is reasonable, it will approve what I do."

144

As she was about to leave, there was a great clatter at the main entrance, and she understood that Octave was arriving. The fatigue induced by the jolting of the journey had caused him to relapse into complete insensibility. Armance, peeping out of a window that gave on to the courtyard, saw between the shoulders of the peasants who carried the stretcher Octave's pale face, quite unconscious. That inanimate head, which lolled back and forth upon the pillow following the movement of the stretcher, was too cruel a spectacle for Armance, who dropped motionless upon the windowsill.

When the surgeons had put the first apparatus in position, and came to report the condition of the wounded man to her as the only member of the family present in the house, they found her silent, staring fixedly at them, unable to reply, and in a state which they considered verging upon madness.

She gave not the slightest credence to all they told her; she believed only what she had seen. Although so reasonable a person, she had lost all self-control. Choked by her sobs, she read through Octave's letter again and again. In the distraction of her anguish she dared to press the letter to her lips in the presence of a lady's-maid. In the re-reading of the letter Armance became aware of the instruction to burn it.

Never was a sacrifice more painful; she must then give up all that remained to her of Octave; but he had wished it. Despite her tears Armance set herself to copy the letter, breaking off at every line to press it to her lips. In the end she steeled herself to burn it upon her little marble-topped table; she gathered up the precious ashes with care.

Octave's servant, the faithful Voreppe, wept by his bedside; he recalled that he had a second letter written by his master : it was the will. This document reminded Armance that she was not the only sufferer. She must go back to Andilly and take the news about Octave to his mother. She went and stood beside the invalid's bed; his extreme pallor and his immobility seemed harbingers of imminent death, although he was yet breathing. To leave him in this condition, in the care of the servants and of a little local surgeon whom she had called in, was the most painful sacrifice of all.

When she reached Andilly Armance found M. Dolier, who had not yet seen Octave's mother; Armance had forgotten that that morning the whole company had made up a party to go to the Château d'Écouen. They had to wait a long time for the return of the ladies, and M. Dolier had time to explain what had happened in the morning; he did not know the nature of the quarrel with M. de Crêveroche.

At last they heard the sound of the horses entering the yard. M. Dolier decided to withdraw, and only to present himself if Mme de Malivert should desire it. Armance, with the least alarmed expression she could muster, announced to Mme de Malivert that her son had had a fall while riding only that morning, and had broken a bone in his right arm. But her sobs, which after the first sentence she could no longer hold back, gave the lie to her tale at every word.

It would be superfluous to describe Mme de Malivert's despair; the poor Marquis was prostrated. Mme de Bonnivet, very upset herself, insisted on returning to Paris in their wake, but was quite unable to cheer him up at all. Mme d'Aumale had fled at the first word of Octave's accident, and was making for the Clichy gate at a gallop; she reached the Rue Saint-Dominique long before the family, learned the whole truth from Octave's servant, and disappeared when she heard Mme de Malivert's carriage stopping at the door.

The surgeons had said that in the patient's extremely weak condition all strong emotion must be carefully avoided. Mme de Malivert moved behind her son's bed in such a way as to see him without being seen.

She hastened to call in her friend the famous surgeon Duquerrel; on the first day this skilful man spoke promisingly of Octave's wound; the household began to hope. As for Armance, she had been struck in the very first instant, and never entertained the slightest delusion. Octave, not being able to speak to her in the presence of so many witnesses, once tried to squeeze her hand.

On the fifth day tetanus developed. At a moment when an access of fever lent him strength, Octave begged M. Duquerrel very earnestly to tell him the whole truth.

The surgeon, a man of true courage, and one who had himself been wounded more than once on the battlefield by Cossack spears, replied :

"Sir, I shall not conceal from you that you are in some danger, but I have seen more than one wounded man in your condition resisting tetanus."

"What proportion of them do?" pursued Octave.

"Since you wish to finish like a man," said M. Duquerrel, "there's a two to one chance that in three days you will be suffering no more; if you have a reconciliation to make with heaven, now is the time for it."

Octave remained thoughtful after this announcement; but soon a feeling of joy and a very obvious smile succeeded his reflectiveness. The excellent Duquerrel was alarmed by the joy, which he took to be a first symptom of delirium.

CHAPTER XXIII

*Tu sei un niente, o morte! Ma sarebbe mai
dopo sceso il primo gradino della mia tomba,
che mi verrebbe dato di veder la vita come
ella é realmente?*   *Guasco*

U P TO that moment Armance had not seen her cousin except in his mother's presence. That day, after the surgeon had left, Mme de Malivert thought to read in Octave's eyes an unusual energy and a wish to talk to Mlle de Zohiloff. She begged her young relative to take her place for a little beside her son, while she went into the next room where she had to write a note.

Octave followed his mother with his eyes; as soon as she was out of sight, he began :

"Armance, my dearest, I am going to die; such a moment holds certain privileges, and you won't be offended by what I am about to tell you for the first time in my life; I shall die as I have lived, loving you passionately; and death is sweet to me, since it allows me to make this confession to you."

The shock prevented Armance from replying; tears brimmed in her eyes, and strange to say they were tears of happiness.

"The most devoted and tender friendship," she told him at last, "binds my destiny to yours."

"I understand," replied Octave, "and I am doubly happy to die. You grant me your friendship, but your heart belongs to another, to that happy man who has been promised your hand."

148

Octave's tone was surfeited with misery; Armance had not the courage to add to his distress at that supreme moment.

"No, my dear cousin," she said, "I can feel nothing more for you than friendship; but no one on earth is more dear to me than yourself."

"And the marriage of which you spoke to me ...?" asked Octave.

"In all my life, I have permitted myself only that one lie, and I beg you to forgive it me. It was the only way I could see of resisting a plan inspired in Mme de Malivert by her excessive prejudice in my favour. I shall never be her daughter, but I shall never love anyone any more than I love you; it is for you, cousin, to decide if you want my friendship at that price."

"If I were destined to live, I should be happy."

"I have one more condition to make," added Armance. "So that I dare unconstrainedly savour the happiness of being perfectly sincere with you, promise me that if heaven grants us your recovery there will never be any question of marriage between us."

"What a strange proviso!" said Octave. "Will you swear to me once again that you are in love with no one?"

"I swear to you," replied Armance, her eyes full of tears, "that in all my life I have never loved anyone but Octave, and that he is far and away what I cherish most in all the world; but I can feel nothing but friendship for him," she added, blushing hotly at the word she had just let slip, "and I shall never be able to repose my trust in him unless he gives me his word of honour that whatever happens, throughout his life, he will make no move, direct or indirect, to obtain my hand."

"I give you my word," said Octave in the greatest astonishment. "But ... will Armance allow me to speak to her of my love?"

"That shall be the name you give to our friendship," said Armance with a bewitching glance.

"It is only for the last few days," said Octave, "that I have

149

known I love you. This is not to deny that, for a long time previously, never five minutes could go by without the memory of Armance interposing to decide whether I ought to think myself happy or unhappy; but I was blind.

"A moment after our conversation in the wood at Andilly a jest of Mme d'Aumale's proved to me that I loved you. That same night I suffered the worst torments of despair; I thought it must be my duty to run away from you; I resolved to forget you and go. In the morning, as I came back in from the forest, I met you in the château garden, and spoke harshly to you, intending that your just indignation at such atrocious behaviour should strengthen my resistance to the sentiment that held me to remain in France. Had you spoken a single one of the gentle words you once were wont to use with me; or had you gazed at me, I should never have found the necessary courage to leave. Do you forgive me?"

"You made me very unhappy, but I had forgiven you before the confession you have just made to me."

It was an hour now since for the first time in his life Octave had begun to savour the happiness of talking to the being he loved about his love.

A single word had just changed the position of Octave and Armance completely, and as thinking of each other had for a long time past filled every moment of their existence, a spellbound astonishment made them forget how near death was; they could not speak a word without discovering new reasons to love each other.

Several times Mme de Malivert tiptoed up to the door of her room. She had not been noticed at all by two beings who had forgotten everything, even cruel death itself, waiting to separate them. She feared, in the end, that Octave's agitation might increase the danger; she came in and said to them almost laughingly : "Do you know, my children, that you have been talking for more than an hour and a half; and it might make your fever worse."

"Mother dear," replied Octave, "I assure you I haven't felt so well in the last four days." He turned to Armance. "One thing distresses me when my fever is very bad. That poor Marquis de Crêveroche had a very handsome dog which used to seem very attached to him. I'm afraid the poor beast may be neglected now that its master is no more. Couldn't Voreppe disguise himself as a poacher and go and buy the beautiful hound? I should at least like to know it's well looked after. I hope I shall see it. At all events, I make you a present of it, my dear cousin."

After such a disturbed day as this Octave fell into a deep sleep, but the following day tetanus developed again. M. Duquerrel felt obliged to speak to the Marquis, and the household was in the depths of despair. Despite his unbending character Octave was dear to the servants; they liked his firmness and fairness.

Though he was often in atrocious pain he was happier than he had ever been in his life before, and the approach of the end of that life caused him to judge it reasonably at last, in a way that redoubled his love for Armance. It was to her that he owed the few happy moments he could perceive in the midst of that ocean of misfortunes and bitter sensations. Upon her advice, instead of standing aloof from the world he had acted, and had rid himself of a great number of false judgments that contributed to his wretchedness. Octave suffered greatly, but to the good Duquerrel's great surprise he stayed alive, and even had some strength.

It took him eight days to renounce his vow that he would never love, which had been the great concern of his whole life. The nearness of death led him first to forgive himself sincerely for breaking that vow. "One dies as one can," he told himself, "and I am dying at the pinnacle of happiness; perhaps chance owed me that compensation after having made me such a constantly wretched being.

"But I may live," he thought, and then he grew more

151

embarrassed. At last he reached the point of telling himself that in the unlikely event of his surviving his wounds the lack of character would consist, not in violating, but in keeping the rash vow he had made in his youth. "Because, after all, the vow was made only in the interests of my happiness and my honour. Why, if I live, should I not continue in Armance's company to taste the sweets of the tender friendship she has sworn me? Is it within my power not to feel the passionate love I bear her?"

Octave was surprised to be alive; when at last, after eight days of conflict, he had resolved all the problems that beset his soul, and had entirely resigned himself to accepting the unexpected happiness heaven had sent him, his condition changed quite completely in twenty-four hours, and the most pessimistic doctors dared to answer to Mme de Malivert for her son's life. Shortly afterwards the fever abated, and he became exceedingly weak, so that he was almost unable to speak.

As he made his way back to life, Octave was seized by lasting amazement; everything had changed for him. "It seems to me," he said to Armance, "that before this accident I was mad. At every moment I used to be thinking of you, and I possessed the art of extracting unhappiness from this charming idea. Instead of adapting my behaviour to the events that occurred in my daily life, I had made myself a rule prior to any experience."

"That's bad philosophy indeed," said Armance laughing; "there's the reason why my aunt positively insisted upon converting you. You are really mad through excess of pride, you gentlemen of great wisdom; I don't know why we prefer you, for you are not at all gay. For my part I am vexed with myself for not feeling friendship towards some scatter-brained young man who talks of nothing but his tilbury."

Once he had fully recovered his faculties Octave did indeed reproach himself a little further for having broken his vows; a little of his self-esteem was lost. But the happiness of telling

152

Mlle de Zohiloff everything, even to the remorse he felt at loving her passionately, placed him who had never before confided in anyone into a state of bliss so far above anything he had ever imagined that he never seriously entertained any thought of resuming his former prejudices and sorrow.

"When I promised myself that I should never fall in love I imposed a task upon myself which is beyond the power of humanity; so that I was constantly unhappy. And this violent state lasted five years! I have found a heart such as I never in the least conceived could exist on earth. Chance, frustrating my folly, sets me face to face with happiness, and I take offence at it, I am almost angry with it! In what way am I acting dishonourably? Who has known of my vow that might now reproach me for violating it? But forgetting one's promises is a contemptible habit; is it nothing, then, to have reason to blush inwardly? But this is a vicious circle; haven't I given myself excellent reasons for breaking the rash promise made by a child of sixteen? The existence of a heart like Armance's answers everything."

Yet such is the sway of an old habit that Octave was never perfectly happy except beside his cousin. He needed her presence.

One doubt sometimes crept in to disturb Armance's happiness. It seemed to her that Octave was not taking her fully into his confidence about the motives which had urged him to flee from her and to leave France after the night spent in the Andilly woods. She considered it beneath her dignity to ask questions, but she said to him one day, quite sternly: "If you wish me to surrender to the inclination I feel I have towards being very friendly with you, you must reassure me against the fear that you will suddenly desert me because of some queer idea that happens to enter your head. Promise me never to leave the place where I am with you, no matter whether it be Paris or Andilly, without giving me *all* your motives." Octave promised.

153

The sixtieth day after he had been wounded he was able to get up, and the Marquise, who felt Mlle de Zohiloff's absence keenly, asked Mme de Malivert to let her come back. Mme de Malivert was in a way pleased to see her go.

One is less circumspect in the intimacy of the domestic circle, and during the anxiety of a great affliction. The brilliant veneer of perfect politeness is less evident at such times, and the true qualities of the soul regain their full ascendancy. His young relative's lack of fortune, and her foreign name which he always took care to mispronounce, had led the Commandeur de Soubirane—and even, occasionally, M. de Malivert—to address her rather as if she were a lady companion.

Mme de Malivert trembled lest Octave should notice it. The respect which kept him silent in his father's case would only have increased the hauteur with which he would have treated the matter in M. de Soubirane's, and the Commandeur's tetchy amour-propre would certainly have revenged itself by spreading some tiresome story concerning Mlle de Zohiloff.

This gossip might come back to Octave's ears, and with the violence of his character Mme de Malivert foresaw the most painful scenes, which might perhaps be most difficult to cover up. Fortunately, nothing her somewhat lively imagination had conjured up did happen; Octave had not noticed anything. Armance had equalized her score with M. de Soubirane by certain indirect epigrams upon the eagerness with which the Knights of Malta had recently been waging war on the Turks, while the Russian officers, their names more or less unknown to history, were taking Ismailoff.

Mme de Malivert, with an eye to the future interests of her daughter-in-law, and to the enormous disadvantage of entering society without fortune and without a name, let slip to a few intimate friends certain confidences intended to discredit in advance all that wounded pride might inspire from M. de Soubirane. These excessive precautions might perhaps not have been out of place; but the Commandeur, who had been gambling on the Bourse since his sister's indemnity, and who only speculated on *complete certainties,* suffered quite a considerable loss, which made him forget his passing inclination to hatred.

After Armance had gone, Octave, who no longer saw her except in the presence of Mme de Bonnivet, was filled with sombre thoughts; his mind was once again dwelling upon his former vow. As the wound in his arm was giving him constant pain, and even sometimes made him feverish, the doctors suggested sending him to take the waters at Barèges; but M. Duquerrel, who knew that not all his patients must be treated alike, claimed that a mildly bracing air would suffice for the patient's recovery, and ordered him to spend the autumn upon the slopes of Andilly.

This spot was dear to Octave; the very next day he was settled there. It was not that he had any hope of seeing Armance; Mme de Bonnivet had been talking for some time about a journey to the depths of Poitou. At great expense she was having restorations carried out at the ancient château where Admiral de Bonnivet had long ago had the honour to entertain François I, and Mlle de Zohiloff was to accompany her.

But the Marquise was secretly informed of a forthcoming promotion within the Order of the Holy Ghost. The late king had promised M. de Bonnivet the blue ribbon. Consequently the architect in Poitou shortly wrote to say that Madame's presence would be purposeless at that moment, because they were lacking workmen, and a few days after Octave's arrival Mme de Bonnivet returned to residence at Andilly.

CHAPTER XXIV

A S THE noise of the servants occupying the attic rooms might have disturbed Octave, Mme de Bonnivet lodged them in a neighbouring peasant's house. It was in this kind of so to speak material consideration that the genius of the Marquise triumphed; she did it with perfect grace, and was very clever at using her fortune to extend the reputation of her intelligence.

The core of her circle consisted of those people who for forty years have done nothing except what is utterly conventional, people who make fashion and then are surprised at it. They declared that if Mme de Bonnivet was self-sacrificing enough not to visit her estates, and to spend the autumn at Andilly to keep her close friend Mme de Malivert company, then it was the bounden duty of every person of sensibility to come and share her solitude.

This solitude was of such a kind that the Marquise was obliged to take rooms in the little village half way up the hill in order to accommodate the friends who were crowding to her side. She had these rooms papered, and had beds installed. Soon half the village had been decorated on her instructions, and was occupied. People were vying with each other for lodgings, and were writing to her from all the châteaux around Paris to ask for a room. It became the done thing to come and keep her company, this admirable Marquise who was looking after poor Mme de Malivert, and during the month of September the village of Andilly was as brilliant as a little spa. The fashion for it was mentioned even at court. "If we had twenty women of intelligence like Mme de Bonnivet," said somebody,

156

"one could risk going to live at Versailles." And M. de Bonnivet's blue ribbon seemed a certainty.

Never had Octave been so happy. The Duchesse d'Ancre found this happiness quite natural. "Octave," she said, "may in some sense regard himself as the centre of all this commotion in Andilly : each morning everyone sends to ask after his health; what could be more flattering at his age? The little fellow's very fortunate," added the Duchesse; "all Paris will be acquainted with him, and that will increase his impertinence by half." This was not precisely where the reason for Octave's happiness lay.

He could see that the beloved mother whom he had so much worried of late was perfectly happy. She was enjoying the brilliant way in which her son was making his début in society. Since his successes, she had begun to give up concealing from herself that his brand of merit was too individual, too little modelled upon well-known merits, to do without the support of the all-powerful influence of fashion. Deprived of this assistance it would have passed unnoticed.

One of Mme de Malivert's happiest occasions at that period was a talk she had with the famous Prince de R ***, who came and spent twenty-four hours at the château d'Andilly.

This shrewd courtier, whose flashes of insight became law in society, appeared to take notice of Octave.

"Have you observed, as I have, Madame," he said to Mme de Malivert, "that your son never repeats a word of that *rehearsed wit* which is the mockery of our time? He disdains, in a salon, to introduce himself with his memory, and his wit depends upon the feelings which are awakened within him. That is why fools are sometimes so displeased with him, and why he lacks their approval. When someone interests the Vicomte de Malivert, his wit seems to spurt suddenly from his heart or from his character, a character which seems to me to be among the finest. Do you not think, Madame, that the

157

character is a worn-out organ in the men of our century? In my opinion your son seems called upon to play a quite particular role. He will have precisely the rarest merit among his contemporaries : there's more in him, there's patently more in him, than in anyone else I know. I should like to see him come to a peerage early, or that you help him to become *Maître des Requêtes."*

"But," protested Mme de Malivert, almost breathless with pleasure at the approbation of so good a judge, "Octave's success is not exactly universal."

"All the better," replied M. de R *** smiling; "it will take the simpletons of this country perhaps three or four years to understand Octave, and before the advent of envy you will be able to push him quite near his place; I ask you only one thing : do not let your son publish; he's too well-born for that."

The Vicomte de Malivert had a long way to go before being worthy of the brilliant future that was being predicted for him; he had a good many prejudices to conquer. His distaste for all men was deeply rooted in his soul; happy, they bred aloofness in him; unhappy, the sight of them was an even greater burden. Only rarely had he been able to try to cure this distaste by good deeds. Had he succeeded in this, a boundless ambition would have thrust him into the midst of men, and into places where glory is won at the price of the greatest sacrifices.

At the period we have now reached, Octave was by no means promising himself brilliant destinies. Mme de Malivert had had the good sense to say nothing to him of the strange future predicted for him by M. le Prince de R ***; it was only with Armance that she dared to surrender to the happiness of discussing this prediction.

Armance possessed the supreme art of relieving Octave's spirit of all the sorrows which the world imposed on him. Now that he dared admit them to her, she was growing more and more surprised at his unusual character. There were still days when he drew the most melancholy conclusions from the most harmless remarks. There was a good deal of talk about him in Andilly. "You are suffering the immediate consequences of fame," Armance told him; "people are saying a great many stupid things about you. Do you expect a fool, merely because he has the honour to be speaking of you, to produce intelligent comments?" It was a singular ordeal for a man quick to take offence.

Armance insisted that he should impart to her completely and promptly every remark offensive to him which he might overhear in society. She easily proved to him that there had been no thought of him when the remarks were made, or that they displayed no more than the degree of ill-will which all the world bears its neighbour.

Octave's self-esteem no longer held any secrets for Armance, and the two young hearts had reached that boundless trust which is perhaps the sweetest delight of love. There was nothing in the world they could speak of without drawing a secret comparison between the delight of their present trust and their constraint of a few months earlier as they talked of the same things. And that constraint whose memory was so sharp—that constraint despite which at that time they were already so happy—was itself a proof of the duration and liveliness of their friendship.

That next day when Octave arrived at Andilly, he was not without some hope that Armance would come there too; he pleaded indisposition and did not leave the château. A few days later Armance did indeed arrive with Mme de Bonnivet. Octave arranged matters so that he should take his first walk outside at precisely seven o'clock in the morning. Armance met him in the garden, and he led her near an orange tree that stood beneath his mother's windows. Here, a few months earlier, Armance, her heart rent by the strange words he was speaking to her, had fallen in a momentary swoon. She recognized the tree, smiled, and leant against the tub of it, closing her eyes. Save for the pallor, she was almost as beautiful as on

159

the day when she had been faint for love of him. Octave was keenly aware of the change in the situation. He recognized the little diamond cross which Armance had had from Russia, and which was an offering of her mother's. Usually it lay hidden, but Armance's movement brought it into view. For a moment Octave lost his head; he took her hand as he had done on the day she fainted, and his lips ventured to brush across her cheek. Armance stood upright with a start and blushed deeply. She reproached herself bitterly for this trifling. "Do you wish to displease me?" she asked him. "Would you force me never to come out without a lady's-maid?"

Several days' coolness was the result of Octave's indiscretion. But between two beings whose attachment to each other was perfect, bones of contention were rare; whatever step Octave was to take, before considering whether it would be pleasant for himself he would try to guess whether Armance might see in it a new proof of his devotion.

In the evening, when they were at opposite ends of the immense drawing-room where Mme de Bonnivet used to gather together all the most notable and influential people of Paris at that time, if Octave had to reply to a question he would make use of a certain word that Armance had just uttered, and she saw that the pleasure of repeating the word would cause him to forget the interest he might have been taking in what he said. All uncontrived there would grow between them in this way, amidst the most pleasant and animated company, something which was not a private conversation but more like an echo, which without expressing anything very distinctly nevertheless seemed to speak of perfect friendship and boundless sympathy.

Dare we charge it with being a little arid, this extreme politeness which the present day believes it has inherited from that happy eighteenth century where there was nothing to hate?

Where such an advanced civilization is present—one which

for every action, however unimportant, undertakes to provide you with a pattern that must be followed, or at the least that must be criticized—this sentiment of sincere and boundless devotion is very close to bringing perfect happiness.

Armance never found herself alone with her cousin except when they walked in the garden in full view of the windows of the château, whose ground floor was in use, or in Mme de Malivert's room when she was present. But this room was a very large one, and often Mme de Malivert's poor health led her to require a few moments' rest; at such times she would urge her children, as she always called them, to go and settle themselves in the recess of the window giving upon the garden, so that the sound of their conversation would not disturb her rest. This peaceful and entirely intimate way of life in the mornings gave place every evening to the very grandest of high society.

Besides the company lodging in the village, many carriages would arrive from Paris, and return after supper. Those cloudless days passed swiftly. Those hearts, still very young, were far from recognizing that they were enjoying one of the rarest happinesses that can be met with on this earth; they believed on the contrary that there were yet many things they desired. Having no experience, they did not see that those fortunate moments could last but a very short time. At best this happiness, compounded entirely of feeling, to which vanity and ambition contributed nothing, might have been able to subsist in the bosom of some needy family that saw no one. But they lived in high society, they were only twenty, they were spending all their time together, and—crowning imprudence—it could be guessed that they were happy, and they looked as though they paid very little heed to society. Society was bound to revenge itself.

Armance had no thought of this peril. Her only anxiety was the necessity, from time to time, to renew to herself the vow never to accept her cousin's hand, whatever might befall. Mme

161

de Malivert, for her part, was quite content; she had no doubt that her son's way of life at that time was leading to an event she wished for passionately.

Despite the happy days with which Armance was filling Octave's life he knew more sombre moments, in her absence, when he would muse upon his destiny, and he arrived at this conclusion: "In Armance's heart reigns the illusion most to my advantage. I could admit the strangest things about myself to her, and far from despising me or being horrified she would be sorry for me."

Octave told his friend that in his early youth he had had a passionate urge to steal. Armance was aghast at the dreadful details into which Octave's imagination was pleased to go concerning the tragic consequences of this strange weakness. This admission overwhelmed her whole existence; she fell into a deep reverie for which she was much upbraided; but hardly had a week gone by since the strange confession, when she had begun to feel pity for Octave and was, if possible, even gentler towards him. "He needs the consolations I can give him," she told herself, "in order to forgive himself."

This experiment assured Octave of the boundless devotion of his beloved, and having no further need to conceal gloomy thoughts he became much more pleasant in society. Before the confession of his love induced by the proximity of death he had been a very witty young man, rather noteworthy than pleasant; he was attractive chiefly to melancholy people. They thought to see in him the *workaday exterior* of a man with a vocation to perform great things. The idea of duty was too apparent in his behaviour, and at times it went so far as to give him an English physiognomy. His misanthropy passed for haughtiness and ill-humour among the older members of society, and shunned all thought of winning their favour. If he had been a peer at this time he would have had quite a reputation.

It is the schooling of misfortune that is often lacking in the pleasant. Octave had just been shaped by the lessons of that terrible master. It is safe to say that at the period we are discussing nothing was lacking to the young Vicomte's comeliness or to the brilliant position he occupied in society. Mme d'Aumale, Mme de Bonnivet and older folk vied with one another in extolling him there.

Mme d'Aumale was right to call him the most attractive man she had ever met, "for he's never tedious," she said carelessly. "Before I met him, I never even dreamed of that kind of merit, and the great thing is to be entertained."

"And I," Armance told herself as she listened to this naïve statement, "I refuse this man permission to press my hand, this man so welcome everywhere else; it's my duty," she added with a sigh, "and I'll never fail in it." There were evenings when Octave indulged in the supreme happiness of remaining silent and watching Armance as she moved before his eyes. These moments were lost neither upon Mme d'Aumale, who was piqued that no one was entertaining her, nor upon Armance, who was enraptured to see the man she adored paying attention to her alone.

The promotion within the Order of the Holy Ghost seemed to be delayed; there was talk of Mme de Bonnivet's leaving for the old château in the depths of Poitou which gave its name to the family. A new character was to travel on this journey, M. le Chevalier de Bonnivet, the youngest son of the Marquis by a first marriage.

CHAPTER XXV

Totus mundus stult.
HUNGARIAE R . . .

A T ABOUT the time of Octave's wound, a new character had arrived from Saint-Acheul to join the Marquise's circle. This was the Chevalier de Bonnivet, her husband's third son.

Had the old Régime still been in existence he would have been destined for the episcopal order, and even though many things have altered, a kind of family habit had persuaded everyone—and himself—that he ought to belong to the Church.

The young man, barely twenty years old, was reputed to be very learned; above all he displayed a sagacity quite beyond his years. He was slight and very pale; he had a chubby face and in all, something of the look of a priest about him.

One evening they brought in the *Etoile*. The single paper band which seals this newssheet was awry; it was clear that the porter had been reading it. "And even this newspaper!" the Chevalier de Bonnivet burst out involuntarily; "to achieve the wretched saving of a second grey paper band which would cross the other one at right angles, it doesn't shrink from the risk that the people will read it, as if the people were made for reading! As if the people could distinguish good from evil! What are we to expect from Jacobin papers when we see the monarchist sheets behaving in this way?"

This burst of involuntary eloquence earned the Chevalier a

great deal of honour. It reconciled the older people to him immediately, and all that part of Andilly society which was more pretentious than intelligent. The taciturn Baron de Risset, whom the reader will scarcely remember, rose solemnly to his feet and embraced the Chevalier without saying a word. For several minutes this action spread an air of solemnity throughout the salon, and amused Mme d'Aumale. She called the Chevalier to her, tried to make him talk, and took him to some extent under her wing.

All the young women followed suit. The Chevalier was turned into a kind of rival for Octave, who was at that time wounded and kept to his room, in Paris.

But soon people began to feel in some way repelled by the Chevalier de Bonnivet, despite his youth. One sensed in him a singular lack of sympathy for all that interests us; he was a young man with a future apart. One perceived something within him fundamentally treacherous towards all existence.

The day after the one when he had shone at the expense of the *Etoile*, the Chevalier de Bonnivet, meeting Mme d'Aumale early in the morning, opened the conversation with her rather like Tartuffe when he offers Dorine a handkerchief so that she may cover up *things which should not be seen*. He reprimanded her in all seriousness upon I know not what idle remark which she had just let fall about a procession.

The young Comtesse retorted briskly, urged him at some length to come back, and was entranced by this absurdity. "It's exactly like my husband," she thought. "What a shame that poor Octave isn't here; how we should laugh!"

The Chevalier de Bonnivet was particularly shocked by the sort of glamour which attached to the Vicomte de Malivert, whose name he heard upon everyone's lips. Octave arrived at Andilly and began once more to appear in society. The Chevalier believed him to be in love with Mme d'Aumale, and upon this thought he himself formed the intention of contracting a passion for the pretty Comtesse, in whose presence he was exceedingly affable.

The chevalier's conversation was a ceaseless and highly witty allusion to the major works of the great writers and poets in French and Latin literature. Mme d'Aumale, who had little learning, insisted on having the allusion explained to her, and nothing would amuse her more. The Chevalier's genuinely prodigious memory served him well; he could recite without hesitation the lines of Racine or the sentences of Bossuet which he had wished to recall, and he would show clearly and elegantly in what way the allusion he had wished to make was relevant to the subject of the conversation. In Mme d'Aumale's eyes all this had the charm of novelty.

One day the Chevalier said: "One single little article in *La Pandore* is designed to spoil all the pleasure that power affords." This passed as being very profound.

Mme d'Aumale strongly admired the Chevalier; but after no more than a few weeks he made her afraid. "You have the same effect on me," she told him, "as a venomous beast I might meet in a lonely spot in the depths of the forest. The cleverer you are the more power you have to do me harm."

Another day she told him she would wager he had guessed this great principle all by himself: that speech was granted to man to conceal his thoughts.

The Chevalier was a great success with other people in society. For example, although he had been away from his father for eight years, spent at Saint-Acheul, Brigg, and other places often unknown even to the Marquis himself, hardly had he returned to his side than he succeeded, in less than two months, in taking complete possession of the mind of the old man, who was one of the subtlest courtiers of the time.

M. de Bonnivet had always been afraid lest France's Restoration might finish as England's had; but for the last year or two this fear had turned him into a thorough miser. Everyone in society was greatly surprised, therefore, to see him hand over thirty thousand francs to his son the Chevalier toward the establishment of certain Jesuit houses.

Every evening, in Andilly, the Chevalier conducted prayers for the forty or fifty servants belonging to the people who were staying at the château or lodging in the peasant houses that were arranged for the Marquise's friends. These prayers were followed by a short sermon, impromptu and exceedingly well-turned.

At first the older women began to go to the orangery, where this evening exercise took place. The Chevalier had lovely flowers put there which were brought from Paris and frequently renewed. Soon this pious and severe exhortation aroused general interest; it contrasted sharply with the frivolous way in which the rest of the evening was spent.

The Commandeur de Soubirane declared himself one of the warmest supporters of this means of redeeming to sound principles all the underlings who of necessity surround eminent people, and who, he added, showed such cruelty at the first onset of the Reign of Terror. This was one of the Commandeur's habits in conversation, and he used to go about proclaiming that within ten years, if the Orders of Malta and the Jesuits were not re-established, there would be a second Robespierre.

Mme de Bonnivet had not omitted to send to her stepson's pious exercises those of her domestic staff whom she trusted. She was surprised to learn that he was distributing money to servants who came and confided to him privately that they were in need.

As the promotion in the Order of the Holy Ghost seemed to have been deferred, Mme de Bonnivet announced that her architect had sent her word from Poitou that he had succeeded in assembling a sufficient number of workmen. She made ready for the journey and so did Armance. She was only moderately pleased when the Chevalier announced his intention of accompanying them to Bonnivet, in order, as he put it, to see the ancient château, the cradle of his family, once more.

The Chevalier saw quite clearly that his presence annoyed his stepmother; this to him was one more reason for accompanying her on the journey. He was hoping to impress Armance with the recollection of the glory of his ancestors; for he had noticed that Armance was the friend of the Vicomte de Malivert, and he wanted to take her away from him. These plans, thought out long beforehand, were not apparent until the moment they were carried out.

Being just as successful with young people as with the earnest part of society, the Chevalier de Bonnivet, before leaving Andilly, was skilful enough to inspire Octave with a good deal of jealousy. After Armance's departure Octave went so far as to wonder whether this Chevalier de Bonnivet, who displayed boundless esteem and respect for her, could conceivably be that mysterious husband found for her by an old friend of her mother's.

When they parted from each other, Armance and her cousin were both tormented by dark suspicions. Armance was conscious that she was leaving Octave close to Mme d'Aumale, but she did not feel entitled to write to him.

Throughout this cruel separation all that Octave could do was to send two or three letters to Mme de Bonnivet; they were very charming but oddly phrased. Had someone outside that circle seen them, he would have concluded that Octave was madly in love with Mme de Bonnivet and dared not confess his love to her.

During this month of separation Mlle de Zohiloff, whose common sense was no longer disturbed by the happiness of living under the same roof as her friend and of seeing him three times a day, indulged in some serious thinking. Although her conduct was perfectly proper, she could not shirk the fact that it must be easy to read her thoughts in her eyes when she looked at her cousin.

As it fell out on the journey she happened to overhear certain remarks by Mme de Bonnivet's maids which made her shed bitter tears. These women, like all who have to do with eminent people, saw everywhere no other motive except money, and so ascribed to this motive the outward shows of passion which Armance was affecting, they said, in order to become Vicomtesse de Malivert; which wouldn't be too bad for a poor young lady of such humble lineage.

That she might be the victim of such a degree of calumny had never occurred to Armance. "I am utterly lost," she told herself; "my feeling for Octave is more than suspected, and that's not the worst of the faults I'm supposed to have; I live in the same house as he does, and it's not possible that he will marry me. . . ." From that moment forth the idea of the calumnies of which she was the object resisted all Armance's arguments, and poisoned her existence.

There were moments when she believed she had even forgotten her love for Octave. "Marriage is not for people in my position; I shan't be married to him," she thought, "and I must live much more apart from him. If he forgets me, as it's quite probable he will, I shall go and finish my days in a convent; it will be a very suitable and welcome refuge for the remainder of my existence. I shall think of him, and hear of his successes. Society can call to mind many lives similar to the one I shall lead."

These forethoughts were sound; but a young woman's horror that she might perhaps, with some semblance of justification, be exposed to the calumny of a whole household, worse still the household of which Octave was a member, cast a shadow across Armance's life which nothing could dispel. If she set about escaping from the recollection of her faults—for this was the name she used for the kind of life she had lived at Andilly—her thoughts would dwell on Mme d'Aumale, whose attractions she would overrate unwittingly; the company of the Chevalier de Bonnivet contributed to making her regard as even more irremediable than they really are, all the hurts that society can inflict when one has offended it. Towards the end of her stay at the ancient Château de Bonnivet, Armance spent all her nights in weeping. Her aunt noticed this sadness and did not conceal from her all the annoyance she felt because of it.

It was during her stay in Poitou that Armance learned of an occurrence which affected her but little. She had three uncles in the service of Russia; these three young men committed suicide during the disturbances in that country. Their death was kept secret; but in the end, after several months, letters which the police had been unable to suppress were sent through to Mlle de Zohiloff. She inherited a comfortable fortune, and one which could make her a suitable match for Octave.

This event was not designed to alleviate the ill-humour of Mme de Bonnivet, to whom Armance was a necessity. The poor girl had to endure an exceedingly harsh comment upon the preference she was showing for Mme de Malivert's salon. Great ladies are no more unkind than the common run of wealthy women; but in their company one acquires more susceptibility, and disagreeable remarks are felt more deeply, more irremediably, if I dare put it that way.

Armance believed nothing was lacking to complete her wretchedness, when one morning the Chevalier de Bonnivet, with that indifferent tone that one uses for news already stale, told her that Octave was quite ill again, and that the wound in his arm had reopened, and was giving cause for anxiety. After Armance's departure Octave, who had become hard to please in the matter of happiness, often grew bored in the salon. While out hunting he did one or two imprudent things which had serious consequences. It had occurred to him to shoot with his left hand, using a very light, small gun; he achieved some success, which encouraged him.

One day as he was following up a winged partridge he jumped a ditch and hit his arm against a tree, which caused a renewal of his fever. During this fever and the indisposition which followed it, the so-to-speak artificial happiness he had enjoyed in the sight of Armance seemed no longer to have any more substance than a dream.

At last Mlle de Zohiloff returned to Paris, and the very next day at the château of Andilly the lovers met again, but they were very dejected, and this dejection was of the worst kind, for it emanated from doubts of each other. Armance did not know what attitude to take with her cousin, and they hardly talked to each other at all on the first day.

While Mme de Bonnivet was indulging in the pleasure of building Gothic towers in Poitou, under the impression that she was reconstructing the twelfth century, Mme d'Aumale had taken a decisive step to achieve the great success which had now at last crowned M. de Bonnivet's old ambition. She was the heroine of Andilly. In order not to lose touch with so useful a friend, Mme de Bonnivet had persuaded the Comtesse d'Aumale to agree to occupy a little suite on the top floor of the château just beside Octave's room, during the Marquise's absence. It seemed to everyone that Mme d'Aumale very frequently remembered that it was in a way for her sake that Octave had received the wound which caused his fever. It was in very poor taste indeed to recall the incident, which had cost the Marquis de Crêveroche his life; none the less Mme d'Aumale could not refrain from alluding to it often : the fact is that the manners of society are to delicacy of soul very much what science is to the mind. This character, turned quite to the outside and not at all romantic, was chiefly impressed by things that were real. Hardly had Armance been more than a few hours at Andilly when she was vividly struck by this frequent reference to the same ideas, in one who was usually so fickle.

She was already very sad and discouraged when she arrived; for the second time in her life she felt the stab of a sentiment which is terrible, above all when it occurs in the same heart as the exquisite sentiment of propriety. Armance believed she had a good deal for which to reproach herself on this score. "I must guard myself strictly," she thought, averting her eyes, which were dwelling upon Octave, and turning them towards the brilliant Comtesse d'Aumale. And each of the Comtesse's graces gave Armance fresh cause for humbling herself to excess. "How could Octave fail to prefer her?" she said to herself; "I myself can see that she is adorable."

Such painful feelings, together with the remorse which Armance was suffering—no doubt unjustified, but none the less cruel for that—left her little inclined to be amiable towards Octave. The day after her arrival she did not go down into the garden early, as had been her wont before; and she was well aware that Octave was awaiting her there.

During the day Octave spoke to her two or three times. An extreme shyness, which seized her when she thought that everybody was watching them, left her paralysed, and she barely answered.

That day at dinner the talk turned to the fortune which chance had just bestowed upon Armance, and she noticed that this news was clearly little to Octave's liking; he said not a word to her about it. The word he did not say, had he in fact spoken it to her, would not have kindled pleasure in her heart equal even to a hundredth part of the agony she suffered through his silence.

Octave was not listening; he was thinking how strangely Armance had behaved towards him since her return. "Obviously she is no longer in love with me," he told himself, "or else she has engaged herself definitely to the Chevalier de Bonnivet." Octave's indifference to the news of Armance's fortune broached a new and fathomless spring of misfortunes for the poor girl. For the first time she gave long and serious thought to the inheritance which came to her from the North, and which, had Octave loved her, would have made her a more or less suitable match for him.

Octave, as an excuse for writing a line to her in Poitou, had sent her a little poem about Greece recently published by Lady Nelcombe, a young Englishwoman friendly with Mme de

172

Bonnivet. There were only two copies of the poem in France, and it was much talked of. If the copy which had made the journey to Poitou had appeared in the salon, twenty indiscreet requests would have been proffered to intercept it. Octave begged his cousin to have it sent to his room. Armance, thoroughly nervous, did not feel she had the courage to entrust her maid with such an errand. She went up to the second floor of the château and balanced the little English poem on Octave's doorhandle, in such a way that he could not enter his room without seeing it.

Octave was very disturbed; he could see that Armance most decidedly did not wish to speak to him. As he himself felt in no mood to talk to her either, he left the drawing-room before ten o'clock. A thousand sinister thoughts troubled him. Very soon Mme d'Aumale grew weary of the drawing-room; they were talking politics, and dreary politics too; for her part she spoke of a headache, and before half past ten she had retired to her rooms. Probably Octave and Mme d'Aumale had gone for a walk together; at this thought, which occurred to everybody, Armance turned pale. Then she reproached herself for her sorrow as though it were a solecism which made her less worthy of her cousin's esteem.

Early the following morning Armance was with Mme de Malivert, who had need of a certain hat. Her maid had gone down to the village; Armance ran to the room where the hat was kept; she had to pass Octave's room on the way. She stopped as though stricken by lightning when she saw the little English poem resting on the doorhandle, just as she had put it the evening before. It was clear that Octave had not been to his room.

This was perfectly true. He had gone hunting, despite the latest accident to his arm, and so that he might get up in the morning without being observed he had spent the night at the gamekeeper's. He intended to return to the château at eleven o'clock when the bell rang for the midday meal, and thus escape

173

the reproaches which his imprudence would otherwise have earned him.

When she returned to Mme de Malivert's room, Armance was obliged to say that she felt unwell. From that moment she was no longer the same person. "I am suffering a well-deserved punishment," she told herself, "for the false position in which I have placed myself, one which is so improper for a young woman. Because of it I have come to have sorrows which I can't admit even to myself."

When she saw Octave again, Armance did not have the courage to ask him the most trifling question about what had chanced to prevent his seeing the English poem; she would have thought she was failing in all she owed herself. This third day was even more dismal than those which went before it.

CHAPTER XXVI

OCTAVE, IN consternation at the change he could see in Armance's behaviour, thought that even in his role of friend he might hope that she would tell him the secret of her anxieties; for she was unhappy, Octave could have no doubt of that. It was equally clear to him that the Chevalier de Bonnivet sought to deny them every opportunity to talk together which might have arisen by chance during a walk or in the drawing-room.

The hints which Octave risked from time to time brought no response. For her to admit her grief and throw over the system of perfect self-restraint which she had imposed upon herself, Armance would have had to be deeply, emotionally shaken. Octave was too young and too unhappy himself to discover this fact and profit by it.

The Commandeur de Soubirane had come to dinner at Andilly; in the evening there was a thunderstorm, and it rained in torrents. The Commandeur was persuaded to stay, and was accommodated in a room near the one Octave had just occupied on the second floor of the château. That evening Octave had determined to restore a little of Armance's gaiety; he felt a need to see her smile; and in that smile he would have seen a reflection of their former intimacy. His gaiety failed miserably and much displeased Armance. As she was making no reply he was obliged to address his conversation to Mme d'Aumale, who was present and laughing a great deal, while Armance preserved a bleak silence.

Octave risked embarking on a question which seemed to require quite a long reply; the answer was in two dry words.

175

Disheartened by the conspicuousness of his disgrace, he left the drawing-room instantly. As he was strolling round the garden he met the gamekeeper, whom he told that he would be going hunting early the following morning.

Mme d'Aumale, seeing no one in the drawing-room except earnest people, whose conversation was burdensome to her, made up her mind and disappeared. To poor Armance this was only too clearly a second assignation. Indignant above all at Octave's duplicity—that very evening he had spoken some most tender words to her as he was passing from one room to another—she went up to her room to find a book which it occurred to her she would balance, like the little English poem, on Octave's doorhandle. As she came along the corridor leading to her cousin's room, she heard a noise within; his door was open and he was preparing his gun. There was a tiny closet that served as a hallway to the room which had been got ready for the Commandeur, and the door of this closet gave on the corridor. By an unlucky chance its door was open. Octave moved towards the door of his room and made as if to come out into the corridor. It would have been terrible for Armance to be seen by Octave at that moment. She only just had time to throw herself through the door which stood open beside her. "As soon as Octave has gone out," she thought,

"I'll go and put the book in place." She was so agitated by the thought of what she was daring to do, something very wrong indeed, that she was barely capable of connected thought.

Octave did indeed come out of his room; he passed in front of the open door of the little closet where Armance was; but he only went down to the end of the corridor. He stood at a window and whistled twice, as though giving a signal. The gamekeeper, who was drinking in the pantry, did not reply, and Octave remained at the window. The silence reigning in this part of the château, the company being in the drawing-room on the ground floor and the servants in the basement, was so complete that Armance, whose heart was pounding, dared not make a move. Besides poor Armance could not ignore that Octave had just given a signal; and however unfeminine it might be it seemed to her that Mme d'Aumale might very well have chosen it.

The window on which Octave leant was at the head of the little staircase leading down to the first floor, and it was impossible to pass. Octave whistled a third time just after eleven had struck; the gamekeeper who was in the pantry with the servants did not reply. Towards half past eleven Octave returned to his room.

Armance, who had never in her life engaged in any undertaking for which she ought to blush, was so distressed that she found herself quite unable to walk. It was clear that Octave was giving a signal; someone would reply to it, or he would come out again in a moment. The château clock struck a quarter to twelve; then midnight. This disgraceful hour made Armance feel guiltier than ever; she decided to leave the closet which had served her as shelter, and on the last stroke of midnight she made a move. Although she was normally so light on her feet she was in such a turmoil that she made quite a noise.

As she went down the corridor she saw in the shadows, by the window near the staircase, a figure silhouetted against the sky, and she quickly recognized M. de Soubirane. He was waiting for his servant who was fetching him a candle, and at the moment when Armance, motionless, stood looking at the figure of the Commandeur whom she had just recognized, the rays of the candle, as it started to move up the stairs, began to appear on the corridor ceiling.

Had she been cool Armance might have tried to hide behind a big linen-press that stood in the corner of the corridor by the staircase; in this way she might have been saved. Paralysed with terror, she lost two seconds, and as the servant reached the top step of the stairs the light of the candle fell full upon

177

her, and the Commandeur recognized her. His lips broke into a horrible smile. His suspicions of the understanding between Armance and his nephew were confirmed, but at the same time here was an opportunity for him to ruin them for ever. "Saint-Pierre," he said to his servant, "Is not that Mlle de Zohiloff?" "Yes, sir," said the servant, quite bewildered. "Octave is better, I hope, Mademoiselle?" said the Commandeur in a coarse, jeering voice, and he passed on.

CHAPTER XXVII

ARMANCE, IN despair, saw herself at once dishonoured for ever and betrayed by her lover. She sat down for a moment on the last step of the stairs. It occurred to her to go and knock at the door of Mme de Malivert's maid. The girl was asleep and did not stir. Mme de Malivert, with a vague fear that her son might be ill, took her nightlight and came and opened the door of her room herself; she was frightened by Armance's face. "What's happened to Octave?" cried out Mme de Malivert. "Nothing, Madame, nothing has happened to Octave, he's very well; it's only I who am unhappy and in despair at disturbing your sleep. I had intended to speak to Mme Dérien and only to call on you if I were told you were not yet asleep." "My dear child, you redouble my dread with this word Madame. There is something extraordinary going on. Is Octave ill?" "No, Maman," faltered Armance, bursting into tears, "it's only that I am ruined."

Mme de Malivert made her come into the bedroom, where she related all that had just happened to her, without hiding or omitting a single thing, even her jealousy. Armance's heart, exhausted by so many misfortunes, no longer had the strength to withhold anything.

Mme de Malivert was appalled. Suddenly she cried out: "We mustn't waste any time. Give me my pelisse, my poor child —my dear child," and she kissed her twice or three times with all a mother's passion. "Light my candle; now you stay here." Mme de Malivert ran to her son's room; fortunately the door was unlocked; she slipped in quietly, wakened Octave and told him what had just happened. "My brother can ruin us," said Mme de Malivert, "and judging by appearances fully intends to do so. Will you please get up, go to his room, and tell him I have had some sort of stroke in your room. Can you see any better way?"

"Yes, mother, marry Armance tomorrow, if the angel will still have me."

This unexpected remark gave Mme de Malivert the most heartfelt satisfacton, and she embraced her son; but on second thoughts she added : "Your uncle doesn't like Armance; he may talk; he will promise to be silent, but there is his servant who, on his orders, will talk, and who will immediately afterwards be dismissed for having talked. I am still in favour of my idea of a stroke. It's a farce that will keep us busy disagreeably for three days, but the honour of your wife is more precious than all else. Don't forget that you must seem very frightened. As soon as you have told the Commandeur, go down to my room and explain our idea to Armance. When the Commandeur met her on the stairs, I was in your room and she was on the way to fetch Mme Dérien." Octave ran to tell his uncle whom he found very much awake. The Commandeur looked at him with an air of mockery which changed all his emotion into anger. Octave left M. de Soubirane and flew down to his mother's bedroom : "Is it possible," he said to Armance, "that you are not in love with the Chevalier de Bonnivet, and that he is not the mysterious husband you used once to tell me about?"

"The Chevalier fills me with horror. But you, Octave, aren't you in love with Mme d'Aumale?"

"I shall never see her nor think of her again," said Octave. "Dearest Armance, deign to tell me that you will accept my hand in marriage. Heaven is punishing me for having kept my hunting expeditions a secret from you; I was whistling to the gamekeeper who did not reply." Octave's protestations had all the warmth but not all the delicacy of true passion;

Armance had the impression that he was carrying out a duty while his mind was elsewhere. "You don't love me at this very moment," she told him.

"I love you with all the force of which my soul is capable, but I am carried away by anger against that ignoble Commandeur; a vile man, on whose silence one dare not rely." Octave renewed his entreaties.

"Is it certain this is love that speaks?" asked Armance; "perhaps it's nothing but generosity, and you are in love with Mme d'Aumale. You used to abhor marriage; this sudden conversion seems very suspicious to me."

"In the name of heaven, dear Armance, let's waste no time; all the rest of my life shall answer to you for my love." He spoke with such conviction that in the end she in her turn was convinced. He went quickly back upstairs, and found the Commandeur with his mother, whose joy at Octave's impending marriage was giving her courage to act out her part very plausibly. However the Commandeur did not seem entirely convinced about his sister's attack. He indulged in a jest concerning Armance's nocturnal errands. "Sir, I still have one sound arm," cried Octave, springing up at once and rushing at him; "if you add one word more I shall throw you out of the window—this one here!" The Commandeur turned pale at Octave's curbed fury, and he remembered pertinently his nephew's fits of madness, and saw that he was angered to the point where he might commit a crime.

Armance appeared at that moment, but Octave could find nothing to say to her. He could not even look at her with love; keeping calm had driven him distracted. When the Commandeur, to put a bold face on it, tried to make a few light-hearted remarks, Octave was afraid they might wound Mlle de Zohiloff. "Sir," he said, seizing his arm in a firm grip, "I advise you to retire to your room immediately." As the Commandeur hesitated Octave seized him by the arm, dragged him to his

181

room, threw him in there, locked the door, and put the key in his pocket.

When he returned to the ladies he was furious. "If I don't kill that base, mercenary soul," he cried out as though to himself, "he will dare to speak ill of my wife. The devil take him!"

"For my part I like M. de Soubirane," said Armance, who was frightened and saw how Octave was hurting his mother. "I like M. de Soubirane, and if you go on being furious I might think you are out of temper because of a certain rather sudden engagement which we have just announced to him."

"You don't believe that, I'm sure," interrupted Octave. "But you're right as usual. Properly speaking, I owe a debt of thanks to that vile being," and little by little his anger evaporated. Mme de Malivert had herself carried back to her room, continuing very effectively to act out the fiction of a stroke. She sent to Paris for her doctor.

The rest of the night was delightful. The happy mother's gaiety infected Octave and his friend. Urged on by Mme de Malivert's cheerful comments, Armance, who was still very upset and had lost all dominion over herself, dared to show Octave how dear he was to her. She knew the extreme pleasure of seeing him jealous of the Chevalier de Bonnivet. It was this blessed feeling which explained so happily for her his apparent indifference of the preceding days. Mme d'Aumale and Mme de Bonnivet who had been wakened despite Mme de Malivert's orders, only came in very late, and everyone went to bed at daybreak.

CHAPTER XXVIII

This is the state of man; today he puts forth
The tender leaves of hope, tomorrow blossoms,
And bears his blushing honours thick upon him.
The third day comes a frost, a killing frost;
And then he falls—see his character.
King Henry VIII, Act III

VERY EARLY the following morning Mme de Malivert arrived in Paris to propose Octave's marriage to her husband. He prevaricated all day; "it's not," said the Marquis, "that I haven't been expecting this vexatious suggestion for a long time. It would be quite wrong for me to pretend to be surprised. Mlle de Zohiloff is not totally without fortune, I admit; her Russian uncles died very conveniently for her. But her fortune is no greater than we could find elsewhere, and—something of the greatest consequence to my son—there is no family in this match; I can see nothing in it beyond a dismal similarity of characters. Octave hasn't enough relatives in society, and his way of withdrawing quite within himself brings him no friends. He will be a Peer after his cousin and after myself, and that is all; and as you know, my dear, in France, a man's worth makes the worth of his position. I belong to the old generation, as these insolent puppies say; I shall soon be gone, and with me all the ties that may exist between my son and society; for he's an instrument of our dear Marquise de Bonnivet, but not an object for her. In making a match for Octave we should have been looking for social connections even before wealth. I see in him one of those merits particularly fitted, if you like, to achieve success alone. I have always noticed that such sublime people require to have their praises cried, and my son, far from flattering the makers of reputation, seems to find a malicious pleasure in defying them and insulting them to their faces. That is not the way to succeed. With a numerous and well-established family he might have passed in society as worthy of a ministry; he is blazoned by nobody, and will be no more than an eccentric."

Mme de Malivert protested vehemently against this word. She could see that someone had been *predisposing* her husband.

He resumed more strongly than ever : "No, my dearest one, I shouldn't like to swear that Octave's facility for taking offence, and his passion for what are called principles—now that the Jacobins have changed everything among us, even our language—might not one day land him in the worst of stupidities, into what you call the *opposition*. The only man of importance your opposition ever had, the Comte de Mirabeau, finished by selling himself; it's an ugly outcome, and one that I shouldn't like for my son either."

"And it's also one that you ought not to fear," retorted Mme de Malivert briskly.

"No, it's into the opposite abyss that my son's fortune will topple and disappear. This marriage will turn him into nothing but a bourgeois living cooped up in his château in the depths of his countryside. His gloomy character inclines him only too much already towards that kind of life. Our dear Armance has strange ways of looking at things; far from tending to change what I find reprehensible in Octave, she will lend strength to his bourgeois habits, and you're vitiating our family with this marriage."

"Octave is destined to the House of Peers, and there he will be a noble representative of French youth, and by his eloquence win personal respect."

"He is not alone in that; all these young Peers make pretension to eloquence. 'Pon my soul, in their Chamber they'll be exactly as they are in society—perfectly polite, perfectly informed, and that's all! All these young representatives of French youth will be the deadliest enemies of Octave, who has at least an original way of feeling."

Mme de Malivert returned to Andilly very late, with a charming letter for Armance, in which M. de Malivert requested her hand for Octave.

Although much tired by her day out, Mme de Malivert hastened to call on Mme de Bonnivet, who must not learn of this betrothal except from her. She showed her the letter from M. de Malivert to Armance; she was glad to be taking this precaution against people who might change her husband's mind. Besides, it was a necessary step, since the Marquise was in some measure Armance's guardian. This title held her silent. Mme de Malivert gratefully acknowledged the friendship Mme de Bonnivet evinced for Octave by not seeming entirely to approve of the marriage. The Marquise confined herself to lavish eulogy of Mlle de Zohiloff's character. Mme de Malivert was careful not to forget the approach she had made to Armance several months earlier, and the noble refusal of the young orphan, at that time without fortune.

"Oh, it's not Armance's noble qualities about which my friendship for Octave has need of reassurance," said the Marquise. "She has no connections except through us. These family matches are suitable only among powerfully wealthy bankers; as their principal goal is money, they are sure to find it, and quite without fuss."

"We are moving towards a time," replied Mme de Malivert, "when the favour of the Court, unless one is prepared to purchase it by constant personal attentions, will be no more than a secondary aim for a man of high birth, a Peer of France, and very rich. Look at our friend Lord N *** ; his immense standing in his own country springs from the fact that he nominates

185

eleven members of the House of Commons. And for all that, he never sees the king."

This was also Mme de Malivert's reply to the objections raised by her brother, whose opposition was very much sharper. Furious at the previous evening's scene, and determined not to miss the chance of feigning a passionate anger, he wanted, when he allowed himself to be appeased, to place his nephew under the burden of eternal gratitude.

Octave alone he would have forgiven, since after all he had either to forgive or renounce the dreams of wealth which had been his constant preoccupation for a year. As for the scene in the night, his vanity would have consoled itself, among his intimate circle, with the well-known madness of Octave who used to throw his mother's footmen out of windows.

But the idea of Armance all-powerful over the heart of a husband who loved her to distraction decided M. de Soubirane to declare that he would never in his life set foot again in Andilly. Andilly was delighted, took him at his word to some extent, and after having made all kinds of excuses and advances to him, forgot him.

Since he had perceived himself to be reinforced by the arrival of the Chevalier de Bonnivet, who supplied him with good arguments and, on occasion, whole sentences ready-made, his estrangement from Mlle de Zohiloff had grown into hatred. He could not forgive her her allusions to Russian valour deployed before the walls of Ismailoff, while the Knights of Malta, *sworn* enemies of the Turks, rested upon their rock. The Commandeur might have forgotten an epigram he had provoked; but the fact was, there was *money* at the root of all this anger against Armance. The Commandeur's somewhat feeble mind was absolutely possessed by the idea of making a great fortune on the Bourse. As it happens with all commonplace souls, towards fifty the interest which he took in the things of this world had petered out, and boredom had ensued; again according to custom the Commandeur had wished to be successively a

186

man of letters, political intriguer, and dilettante of the Italian opera. I know not what misunderstanding had prevented him from becoming a Secular Jesuit.

In the end gambling on the Bourse had followed, and had been found a sovereign remedy for limitless tedium. But for gambling on the Bourse he lacked only funds and credit. The indemnity had turned up just at the right moment, and the Commandeur had sworn that he would easily guide his nephew, who was only a philosopher. He firmly intended to take to the Bourse a large part of whatever Octave received for his mother's indemnity.

In the full flush of his passion to make millions, Armance had appeared as an insurmountable obstacle in the Commandeur's way. Now her admission into the family was dissipating for ever both his credit with his nephew and his castles in Spain. The Commandeur was wasting none of his time in Paris, and was going about stirring up trouble against his nephew's marriage, at the houses of Mme la Duchesse de C ***, protectress of the family, Mme la Duchesse d'Ancre, Mme de la Ronze, and Mme de Claix, in whose company he was passing his time. The unsuitability of this alliance was soon agreed upon by all the friends of the family.

In less than a week the young Vicomte's betrothal was known to the whole world and no less generally condemned. The great ladies who had marriageable daughters were furious.

"Mme de Malivert," said the Comtesse de Claix, "is cruelly forcing poor Octave to wed her lady-companion, apparently to save the wages she would have had to pay the girl; it's such a shame."

In the midst of all this the Commandeur believed himself forgotten in Paris where he was dying of boredom. The general outcry against Octave's marriage could not possibly be more lasting than anything else. Advantage must be taken of this universal vehemence while it still existed. Settled betrothals cannot be broken except in very short order.

In the end, in consequence of all these good reasons and boredom most of all, the Commandeur was to be seen one fine morning arriving at Andilly, where he took up his quarters and his ordinary way of life just as if nothing had happened.

The new arrival was treated with great politeness, and he took care to make the most cordial advances to his future niece. "Friendship, no less than love, has its illusions," he said to Armance, "and if at first I found fault with a certain arrangement, it was because I too am passionately fond of Octave."

CHAPTER XXIX

*Ses maux les plus cruels sont ceux qu'il
se fait lui-même.*   *Balzac*

ARMANCE MIGHT have been deceived by these polite
advances, but she did not pause to think about the
Commandeur; she had other causes for anxiety.

Now that there was no longer anything in the way of his
marrying, Octave was having moods of black melancholy
which he could hardly disguise; he would offer the excuse of a
violent headache and go riding alone in the Ecouen and Senlis
woods. Sometimes he would gallop seven or eight leagues at a
stretch. To Armance these symptoms seemed ominous; she
noticed that at certain moments he would look at her with eyes
that reflected more suspicion than love.

It was true that these moods of sombre melancholy often
ended in transports of love and a passionate abandon which
she had never seen in him during *the time of their happiness.*
It was thus that she took to describing, as she wrote to Méry de
Tersan, the time that had elapsed between Octave's wound
and the fatal indiscretion she had committed in hiding within
the closet near the Commandeur's room.

Since her marriage had been announced, Armance had had
the consolation of being able to open her heart to her intimate
friend. Méry, brought up in a thoroughly disunited family
which was constantly tossed by new intrigues, was eminently
capable of giving her sensible advice.

During one of those long strolls she took with Octave around the garden of the château and beneath Mme de Malivert's windows, Armance said to him one day: "Your sadness has something so extraordinary about it that I, who in all the world love you alone, have felt I needed to consult a friend before daring to speak to you as I am going to do now. You were happier before that cruel night when I was so imprudent, and I need not tell you that all my happiness has vanished much more quickly than yours. I have a proposition to make to you: let's return to a state of perfect happiness and to that sweet intimacy which was the bliss of my life from the time I learned you loved me, until this fateful idea of marriage. I will take upon myself all the strangeness of the change. I'll tell the world that I have made a vow never to marry. People will find fault with this idea, and it will lower the opinion which a few friends are kind enough to hold of me; what does that matter to me? Opinion, after all, is only of importance to a rich girl to the extent that she thinks of getting married; now I shall certainly never marry." Octave's only reply was to take her hand, and his eyes flooded with tears. "Oh, my dearest angel," he said to her, "how much more you are worth than I!" The sight of these tears in a man so little given to such weakness, and the simplicity of this remark, drained all Armance's resolution from her.

At last she said to him with an effort: "Answer me, my friend. Accept a proposition which will give me back happiness. We shall spend our lives together none the less." She saw a servant approaching. "The dinner-gong's about to ring," she added in distress; "your father will arrive from Paris, and then I shall have no chance to talk to you, and if I don't talk to you I shall be unhappy and disturbed again all day, for I shall doubt you a little."

"You! Doubt me!" said Octave with a look which for a moment banished all Armance's fears.

After they had walked for a few minutes in silence: "No,

Octave," continued Armance, "I do not doubt you; if I doubted your love I hope that God might grant me grace to die; but the fact is, nevertheless, that you have been less happy since our marriage was agreed."

"I'll speak to you as if to myself," said Octave impetuously. "There are times when I am much happier, because I am certain at last that nothing in the world can separate me from you; I shall be able to see you and talk to you at any time, *but* . . ." he added, and fell into one of those moments of sombre silence which filled Armance with despair.

The fear of the dinner-gong which was about to separate them, perhaps for the rest of the day, gave her courage a second time to interrupt Octave's reverie : "But what, dear friend?" she asked him; "tell me everything; that dreadful *but* will make me a hundred times unhappier than all you could ever add."

"Well then," said Octave, stopping, turning towards her, and watching her intently, no longer as a lover, but in such a way as to see what she was going to think; "you shall know everything; death would be less painful to me than the tale I have to tell you, but then I love you much more than life. Need I swear to you, no longer as your lover (and indeed at that moment his glances were no longer those of a lover), but as a gentleman, and as I would swear it to your respected father had he been preserved to us by the goodness of heaven—need I swear to you that I love you alone of all the world, as I have never loved before, as I shall never love again? To be taken from you would be death for me, and a hundred times worse than death; but I have a dreadful secret which I have never confided to anyone, a secret which will explain to you my fated peculiarities."

As he spoke these faltering words, Octave's features became contracted; there was frenzy in his eyes; it was as though he no longer saw Armance; his lips moved convulsively. Armance, even more unhappy than he, supported herself against the tub

191

of an orange-tree; with a start she recognized the orange-tree as the fatal one beside which she had fainted when Octave spoke harshly to her after the night spent in the woods. Octave had stopped dead before her, as though paralysed with horror, not daring to continue. His frightened eyes stared fixedly in front of him as if he had seen a monster.

"Dear friend," Armance said to him, "I was more miserable when you spoke cruelly to me beside this very orange-tree a few months ago; at that time I had doubts of your love. Doubts, did I say?" she continued passionately; "that fatal day I was certain that you did not love me. Oh my friend, how much happier I am today!"

The ring of truth in these last words of Armance's seemed to lessen the bitter, malignant anguish to which Octave was a prey. Armance, forgetting her usual reserve, pressed his hand with passion, and urged him to speak; Armance's face was at one moment so close to Octave's that he felt the warmth of her breath. This sensation touched him to tenderness; speaking became easy for him.

"Yes, my dear friend," he said, looking at her at last, "I adore you; have no doubts of my love; but what is the man who adores you?—a *monster*."

At these words Octave's tenderness seemed to desert him; all at once he broke into a sort of fury, slipped out of Armance's arms as she tried in vain to hold him back, and fled. Armance remained motionless. At that same moment the luncheon-gong sounded. More dead than alive, she had but to arrive in Mme de Malivert's presence to obtain her permission not to remain at table. Octave's servant came in soon afterwards to say that a business matter had just made it necessary for his master to leave for Paris at a gallop.

Luncheon was silent and chilly; the only person to be happy was the Commandeur. His interest aroused by this simultaneous absence of the two young people, he detected tears of anxiety in his sister's eyes; he knew a moment of joy. It seemed to him

192

that the affair of the marriage wasn't going so well any longer; "they can be broken when they're further gone than this one," he told himself, and his excessive preoccupation stopped him from being agreeable to Mme d'Aumale and Mme de Bonnivet. The arrival of the Marquis, who had come from Paris despite a fresh touch of gout, and who showed himself much put out when he did not see Octave whom he had forewarned of his visit, added to the Commandeur's joy. "This is a propitious moment," he said to himself, "to let the voice of reason be heard." No sooner was the meal over than Mme d'Aumale and Mme de Bonnivet returned to their rooms, Mme de Malivert went in to see Armance, and the Commandeur was inspired—that is to say happy—for an hour and a quarter, as he set himself to shake his brother-in-law's resolve concerning Octave's marriage.

There was a strong underlying honesty in all that the old Marquis said in reply. "The indemnity belongs to your sister," he told him, "I myself am a pauper. It is this indemnity which puts us in a position to consider an establishment for Octave; your sister, I believe, desires this marriage with Armance more than he does; besides the girl's not without wealth; in all this I can't, as a gentleman, do more than give my advice; it wouldn't do to make use of my authority in this; it would look as though I wished to deprive my wife of the sweet pleasure of passing her life with her intimate friend."

Mme de Malivert had found Armance very distressed, but uncommunicative. Entreated by friendship, Armance spoke rather vaguely of a slight quarrel, such as occasionally arises between those who are the most fond of each other. "I am quite sure Octave was in the wrong," said Mme de Malivert, rising to her feet, "otherwise you would tell me the whole story," and she went out, leaving Armance alone. This was doing her a great kindness. It very soon became clear to her that Octave had committed some great crime, of which, moreover, he was perhaps exaggerating the dreadful consequences;

193

and as a gentleman he didn't want to allow her to link her destiny to that of a murderer, maybe, without acquainting her with the whole truth.

Dare we say that this means of explaining Octave's strangeness restored a kind of tranquillity to his cousin? She went down into the garden with a faint hope that she might meet him. She felt at that moment completely cured of the profound jealousy which Mme d'Aumale had inspired in her; she did not, it is true, admit to herself these grounds for the state of tenderness and happiness in which she found herself. She felt transported by the tenderest and most generous compassion. "If we have to leave France," she told herself, "and go into faraway exile, even in America, why then, we'll go," she thought joyfully, "and the sooner the better." And her imagination strayed into conjectures of complete solitude and desert islands, too romantic and too overworked by novels to be reported here. Neither that day nor the next did Octave appear; only on the evening of the second day did Armance receive a letter dated from Paris. She had never felt happier. The keenest, the most unrestrained passion breathed through the letter. "Ah, if only he had been here at the moment when he wrote," she thought, "he would have confessed everything to me." Octave gave her to understand that he was detained in Paris by the shame he felt at telling her his secret. "It will not be at all moments," he went on, "that I shall have courage to speak that fatal word, even to you, for it might diminish the sentiments you condescend to feel for me and which are everything to me. Do not entreat me upon this subject, my dearest." Armance hastened to send a reply by a servant who was waiting. "Your greatest crime," she wrote to him, "is to stay away from us," and her surprise equalled her joy when, half an hour after she had written, she saw Octave in person, who had come as far as Labarre, near Andilly, to await her reply.

The days which followed were perfectly happy. The illusions of the passion which animated Armance were so strange that

194

she soon found herself accustomed to loving a murderer. It seemed to her that this at least must be the crime of which Octave hesitated to confess himself guilty. Her cousin was too good a speaker to exaggerate his ideas and he had spoken those precise words : *I am a monster.*

In the first love letter she had ever written to him she had promised him not to ask him questions; this oath she held sacred. The letter with which Octave had replied she treasured. She had re-read it twenty times over; she formed the habit of writing every evening to the man who was to be her husband, and as she would have felt a little shy of pronouncing his name before her lady's-maid she hid her first letter in the tub of that orange-tree which Octave surely knew well.

She told him of it in a word one morning as they were all about to sit down to luncheon. He disappeared on the pretext of having to give an order, and Armance knew the indescribable pleasure, when he returned a quarter of an hour later, of seeing an expression of the liveliest happiness and the tenderest gratitude in his eyes.

A few days afterwards Armance ventured to write to him : "I believe you to be guilty of some great crime; it will be the business of our whole life to atone for it, if it can be atoned for; but strangely enough I am perhaps even more tenderly devoted to you than I was before this confession.

"I am sensible of how much the admission must have cost you; it was the first great sacrifice you have ever made for my sake, and I will own to you that it is only since that instant that I have been cured of a horrid feeling which I too hardly dared admit to you. I imagine the very worst. Thus it seems to me that there is no need for you to make me a more detailed confession before a certain ceremony takes place. You will not have deceived me at all, truly you will not. God forgives the penitent, and I am sure you exaggerate your fault; were it as serious as it possibly could be, I who have seen your sufferings should still forgive you. You shall make me a full confession in a year's time, and perhaps then I shall inspire you with less fear. . . . However, I cannot promise to love you more than I do."

Several letters written in this tone of angelic kindness had almost decided Octave that he should, in writing, confide to his friend the secret he owed her; but the shame, the embarrassment of writing such a letter still held him back.

He went to Paris to consult M. Dolier, the relative who had been his second. He knew that M. Dolier had a strong sense of honour, that he was upright, and insufficiently intelligent to compromise with duty or delude himself. Octave asked him whether it was absolutely necessary for him to tell Mlle de Zohiloff a fateful secret which he would have had no hesitation in confessing to Armance's father or tutor before his marriage. He went so far as to show M. Dolier that part of Armance's letter quoted above.

"You cannot absolve yourself of the need to speak," was the gallant officer's reply; "that is your strict duty. You must not take prior advantage of Mlle de Zohiloff's generosity. It would be unworthy of you to deceive anyone, and it would be yet more beneath the noble Octave to deceive a poor orphaned girl, who, among all the men of the family, can perhaps count him alone as her friend."

Octave had said all these things to himself a thousand times, but they took on an entirely new strength when they were uttered by the mouth of a firm and honest man.

Octave believed himself to be hearing the voice of destiny.

He took leave of M. Dolier, vowing to himself that he would write the fateful letter in the first café that he should encounter on his right after leaving his relative's house; he kept his word. He wrote a letter ten lines in length and addressed it to Mlle de Zohiloff at the Château de . . ., near Andilly.

When he came out of the café, he kept his eye open for a letter-box; as chance would have it he did not see one. Soon a remnant of that painful feeling which led him to delay such a confession as long as possible, persuaded him that a letter of such importance ought not to be entrusted to the post; that it would be better to deposit it himself in the orange-tree tub in the garden at Andilly. Octave had not the wit to recognize in the notion of this delay a last illusion of a passion only just tamed.

What was essential, in his position, was not to yield one inch to the reluctance which the stern counsels of M. Dolier had just helped him to overcome. He mounted his horse to carry his letter to Andilly.

Since the morning when the Commandeur had begun to suspect a measure of disagreement between the lovers, the natural fickleness of his character had given place to a fairly constant desire to cause harm.

He had made the Chevalier de Bonnivet his confidant. All the time the Commandeur had hitherto spent dreaming of speculations on the Bourse, and writing down figures in a note-book, he now devoted to seeking ways of breaking up his nephew's marriage.

His plans were at first a little unreasonable; the Chevalier de Bonnivet set right his scheme of attack. He suggested that the Commandeur should have Armance followed, and with the help of a few louis the Commandeur turned all the servants of the household into spies. He was informed that Octave and Armance were writing to each other and hiding their letters inside the tub of an orange-tree with such and such a number.

Such imprudence seemed incredible to the Chevalier de Bonnivet; he left the Commandeur to think it over. Seeing at the end of a week that nothing had occurred to M. de Sou-birane beyond the vulgar notion of reading the words of love between two lovers, he deftly reminded him that, among twenty different fads, he had for six months been interested in the autography of letters; at that time the Commandeur had em-ployed a high skilled tracer. The idea made its appearance in his head, but produced no result. Yet it was lodged beside a very lively hatred.

The Chevalier was most reluctant to risk himself with such a man. His companion's sterility discouraged him. Besides, at the first rebuff he might well admit everything. Fortunately the Chevalier bethought him of a vulgar novel in which the villain has the lovers' writing forged and manufactures false letters. The Commandeur seldom read at all, but had been very fond of fine bindings. The Chevalier resolved to make a last attempt; if he did not succeed he would abandon the Commandeur to all the barrenness of his own resources. One of Thouvenin's workmen, magnificently paid, laboured night and day and put a superb binding about the novel in which the trick of forged letters was used. The Chevalier took this magnificent book, brought it to Andilly, and spilt coffee upon the page where the counterfeiting of letters was explained.

"I am in despair," he told the Commandeur one morning, as he entered his room. "Mme de ***, who is mad about her books, as you know, has had this pitiful novel beautifully bound. I was stupid enough to borrow it from her, and I have stained a page. Could you not—you who have culled or invented astonishing secret ways for everything—could you not show me a way to *manufacture* a new page?" After he had spoken a great deal, and used words *as close as possible* to the idea which he wished to implant, the Chevalier left the volume in the Commandeur's room.

He spoke to him of it at least ten times before M. de Soubirane had the idea of embroiling the two lovers by forged letters.

He was so proud of this that at first he exaggerated its importance; he spoke of it in this vein to the Chevalier, who was horrified by so immoral a device, and left that evening for Paris. Two days later, in conversation with him, the Commandeur reverted to the idea. "Forging a letter is abominable," cried the Chevalier. "Do you love your nephew with an affection so strong that the *end is able to justify the means?*"

198

But the reader is perhaps as tired as we are of these sorry details; details in which we see the gangrened products of the new generation contending with the fickleness of the old.

The Commandeur, still full of pity for the Chevalier's ingenuousness, proved to him that in a more or less desperate cause the surest way to be vanquished was to attempt nothing.

M. de Soubirane unostentatiously collected from his sister's mantelpiece several samples of Armance's writing, and easily obtained from his tracer copies which were difficult to tell from the originals. He was already formulating, for the subversion of Octave's marriage, the most clear-cut theories upon wintertime intrigues, the distractions of the ball, the advantageous propositions which he could arrange to have put to the family. The Chevalier de Bonnivet was lost in wonder at this character. "Were but this man here a minister," he told himself, "the very highest dignities would be mine. But with that disgraceful charter, public discussions, and freedom of the press, such a being would never become a minister, however noble a birth he could boast." At last, after a fortnight of patient waiting, it occurred to the Commandeur to compose a letter from Armance to her intimate friend Méry de Tersan. For the second time the Chevalier was on the verge of giving up the whole affair. M. de Soubirane had spent two days producing a model letter bubbling with wit and crammed with dainty thoughts, reminiscent of those he used to write in 1789.

"Our century is more serious than that," the Chevalier told him; "You should rather be pedantic, earnest, boring. . . . Your letter is charming; the Chevalier de Laclos would not have disowned it, but nowadays it would deceive nobody."

"Nowadays, always nowadays!" retorted the Commandeur; "your Laclos was no more than a conceited ass. I don't know why you young people take him as a model. His characters write like wigmakers . . ." etc., etc.

The Chevalier was delighted with the Commandeur's hatred of M. de Laclos; he stoutly defended the author of *Les Liaisons*

Dangereuses, was utterly routed, and at length obtained a draft of a letter which, although certainly not emphatic or German enough, was at least fairly reasonable. The draft of the letter decided upon after so stormy a discussion was handed by the Commandeur to his handwriting tracer who, believing it was merely a matter of gallantries, objected just enough to ensure he would be well paid, and reproduced Mlle de Zohiloff's handwriting to a nicety. Armance was represented as writing a long letter to her friend Méry de Tersan about her forthcoming marriage to Octave.

All the way to Andilly with the letter he had written following M. Dolier's advice, the idea dominating Octave's mind had been, on arrival, to induce Armance not to read his letter until evening, after they had parted. Octave intended to leave very early the next morning; he was quite sure that Armance would reply. He hoped in this way to lessen a little the embarrassment of a first meeting after such a confession. Octave had resolved upon it only because he considered there was heroism in Armance's attitude of mind. For a long time now he had not detected a quarter of an hour in Armance's life which was not dominated by happiness or grief resulting from the sentiment which held them united. Octave was in no doubt that she felt a violent passion for him. On arriving at Andilly he leapt from his horse, ran to the garden and, as he was hiding his letter beneath a handful of leaves in the corner of the orange-tree tub, he found one there from Armance.

CHAPTER XXX

H E PLUNGED in quickly beneath an avenue of limes so that he could read it without interruption. He saw from the first few lines that this letter was written to Mlle de Méry de Tersan (it was the letter composed by the Commandeur). But the first lines had so disturbed him that he went on, and read: "I don't know how to answer your reproaches. You are right, my dear, I am mad to complain. The present arrangement is from every point of view far above anything that could be hoped for by a poor girl, newly come into some fortune and quite without family to establish and protect her. He is a man of intelligence and of the highest virtue —perhaps he has too much of both for me. Shall I confess it to you? times have changed a good deal; what would have overjoyed me a few months ago is now no more than a duty; has heaven denied me the ability to love with constancy? I am concluding a reasonable and advantageous arrangement, I keep telling myself, but my heart no longer experiences those sweet raptures which used to be given me by the sight of the man who, to my eyes, was the most perfect on earth, the only being worthy to be loved. I can see today that his temper is uneven; but no, why should I accuse him? It is not he that has changed; my whole misfortune is that there should be unevenness in my own heart. I am about to marry in every way advantageously and honourably; but, my dear Méry, I blush to confess it to you, I am no longer marrying the one I loved above all things; I find him serious and sometimes not very amusing, and it is with him that I am about to spend my whole life! Probably in some lonely château in the depths of some province where we shall propagate Mutual Instruction and Vaccination. Perhaps, my dear, I shall look back with regret upon Mme de Bonnivet's salon; who would have thought so six months ago? This strange fickleness in my character is what distresses me most. Isn't Octave the most remarkable young man we met this last winter? But I spent such a sad youth! I should like an amusing husband. Farewell. The day after tomorrow *I am to be allowed* to go to Paris; I shall be at your door at eleven."

Octave stood stunned with horror. Suddenly he awoke as though from a daydream, and ran to recover the letter which he had just placed in the orange-tree tub; he tore it up angrily, and put the pieces in his pocket.

"I needed to find the wildest and deepest passion," he said to himself icily, "before I could be forgiven my fateful secret. Against all reason, against the lifelong oath I have sworn myself, I thought to have met a being who stood above humanity. To be worthy of such an exception would have required charm and gaiety, and these are what I lack. I made a mistake; there is nothing left for me but to die.

"It would no doubt be a sin against honour to make no confession, if I were shackling Mlle de Zohiloff's destiny for ever. But I can give her freedom in a month. She'll be a young widow, rich, very beautiful, no doubt much sought after; and the name Malivert will be worth more to her in finding *an amusing husband* than the as yet little-known name of Zohiloff."

It was in this frame of mind that Octave entered his mother's room where he found Armance who was talking of him and daydreaming of his imminent return; soon she was as pale and almost as unhappy as he was; and yet he had just told his mother that he could not tolerate the delays which were deferring his marriage.

"A good many people would like to upset my happiness," he had added; "I'm certain of it. What need have we of so many preparations? Armance is richer than I, and it's unlikely she will ever lack clothes or jewels. I dare to hope that before the end of the second year of our union she will be gay, happy, enjoying all the pleasures of Paris, and that she will never repent of the step she is about to take. I don't believe she will ever be immured in some old château in the country."

There was something so strange in the tone of Octave's words, and so little in accord with the wish they expressed, that almost simultaneously Armance and Mme de Malivert felt their eyes fill with tears. Armance could scarcely utter in reply: "*Ah, my dear, how cruel you are!*"

Thoroughly annoyed at being unable to simulate happiness, Octave left the room abruptly. His resolve to terminate his marriage by death lent his behaviour something of dryness and cruelty.

After she had wept with Armance over what she called the madness of her son, Mme de Malivert expressed the conclusion that solitude did no good at all to a naturally sombre character. "Do you still love him despite this failing, for which he himself is the first to suffer?" asked Mme de Malivert; "consult your heart, my dear daughter; I don't wish to make you unhappy, and all may still be broken off." "Ah, mother, I believe I love him yet more now that I no longer believe him to be so perfect." "Well then, my child," resumed Mme de Malivert, "I shall have you married within a week. Until then be indulgent towards him; he loves you, you can have no doubt of that. You know what a sense he has of his duty to his family, and yet you have seen his fury when he thought my brother's unpleasant remarks were being aimed at you. Be sweet and kind, my dear, with one who is being made unhappy by some odd prejudice against marriage." Armance, to whom these random words gave such an impression of truth, redoubled her attention and tender devotion towards Octave.

Early next morning Octave arrived in Paris and spent a very large sum of money, nearly two-thirds of all he had at his disposal, buying expensive jewellery, which he arranged to be included in his wedding-gift to his bride.

He visited his father's notary and caused to be added to the marriage contract certain clauses which were extremely advantageous to his future bride, and which, if she were to be widowed, would provide the most brilliant independence for her.

It was with careful attentions of this kind that Octave filled the ten days which elapsed between his discovery of the letter supposed to be Armance's, and his wedding. These days passed more peacefully for Octave than he would have dared to hope. What makes misfortune so agonizing for sensitive souls is a little glimmer of hope which occasionally lingers on.

Octave had none. His decision was made, and, for the resolute soul, however harsh the firm decision, it does away with reflection on one's fate, and demands no more than the courage for scrupulous execution; and that is very little.

More than anything else, when the necessary preparations and arrangements of all kinds allowed him a moment to himself, Octave felt a continuing astonishment: So Mlle de Zohiloff no longer meant anything to him! He had become so accustomed to a firm belief in the eternity of her love and of their intimate relationship that he kept constantly forgetting that everything was changed; he was unable to envisage life without Armance. Almost every morning, he had to remind himself of his misfortune on awakening. This was a cruel moment. But soon the thought of death would come to solace him and restore peace to his heart.

Yet towards the end of that interval of ten days Armance's utter tenderness caused him a few moments of weakness. In the course of their walks alone, believing herself licensed by their impending marriage, Armance once or twice allowed herself to take Octave's hand, which was a very fine one, and to carry it to her lips. This redoubling of tender attentions, of which Octave was acutely aware, and to which, despite himself, he was extremely sensitive, often lent keenness and poignancy to an ache he believed he had overcome.

His imagination dwelt on what those caresses would have been had they come from someone who truly loved him, from Armance, as she was two months earlier, according to her own admission in the fateful letter to Méry de Tersan. "And my want of amiability and gaiety has been enough to stop her love," thought Octave bitterly. "Alas, it was the art of making myself welcome in society that I should have been learning instead of devoting myself to so many vain sciences! What use have they been to me? What use have my successes with Mme d'Aumale been to me? She would have loved me had I wished it. I was not made to earn the favour of the one whom I respect. It seems that a wretched shyness makes me dismal and not very likeable, when I most passionately desire to please.

"Armance has always frightened me. I have never come near her without feeling that I was appearing before the master of my destiny. I should have besought experience, and what I could see happening in the world, for more accurate ideas about the effect an attractive man produces when he wishes to interest a maiden of twenty. . . .

"But all this is henceforward of no use," said Octave with a wry smile, interrupting himself: "my life is ended. *Vixi et quem dederat sortem fortuna peregi**."

In certain moods of sombre depression Octave went so far as to see in Armance's tender behaviour—so little in keeping with the complete reserve which naturally became her—the performance of a disagreeable duty which she was imposing

---

* As she dies, abandoned by Aeneas, Dido cries out: I have lived, and that destiny which fate has marked out for me, I have followed.

on herself. On these occasions nothing could compare with the brusqueness of his behaviour, which genuinely bordered upon the symptoms of madness.

At other times, less unhappy, he would allow himself to be moved by the alluring grace of this girl who was about to become his bride. It would have been difficult indeed to imagine anything more moving and more noble than the caressing behaviour of the girl who was usually so reserved, now doing violence to the habits of a lifetime in the attempt to give back a little peace to the man she loved. She believed him to be the victim of remorse, and at the same time felt a violent passion for him. Now that the chief business of Armance's life was no longer to conceal her love and to reproach herself with it, Octave had become dearer still to her.

One day, as they were out walking towards the Ecouen woods Armance, herself affected by the tender words she was allowing herself to utter, went so far as to say to him—and she was in good faith when she said it : "It sometimes occurs to me to commit a crime equal to yours, so that I might deserve you should fear me no longer." Octave, enticed by the ring of true passion, and understanding her whole thought, stopped to gaze intently at her, and was on the verge of handing her the letter of confession whose fragments he still had about him. As he slipped his hand into his coat pocket he felt the smoother paper of the letter supposed to be addressed to Méry de Tersan and his good intention was chilled.

CHAPTER XXXI

If he be turn'd to earth, let me but give
him one hearty kiss, and you shall put us
both into one coffin.   *Webster*

O CTAVE WAS committed to a great many necessary
moves with his older relatives whom he knew to dis-
approve strongly of his marriage. In ordinary circumstances nothing would have been more painful to him. He
would have left the town houses of his illustrious relatives
wretched and almost in revulsion against happiness. To his
great surprise he noticed as he fulfilled these duties that nothing
was painful to him; the fact was that nothing any longer interested him. He was dead to the world.

Since the inconstancy of Armance, he looked upon mankind
as an alien species. Nothing could move him, the unhappiness
of the virtuous no more than the prosperity of the criminal. A
secret voice whispered to him : these wretches are less wretched
than you.

With an admirable indifference Octave discharged all that
modern civilization has heaped together in the way of stupid
functions in order to spoil a wonderful day. The marriage took
place.

Taking advantage of a custom which is beginning to become
established, Octave left immediately with Armance for the
Malivert estate, in Dauphiné; and in point of fact he took her
to Marseilles. There he informed her that he had made a vow
to go to Greece and show, despite his distaste for military

207

behaviour, that he could wield a sword. Armance had been so happy since her marriage that she consented undespairingly to this temporary separation. Octave himself, unable to shut his eyes to Armance's happiness, suffered the weakness—in his view a very serious one—of postponing his departure for a week, which he spent with her in visiting La Sainte Baume, the Château Borelli and the country around Marseilles. His heart was softened by the happiness of his young bride. "She's acting a part," he thought to himself, "and her letter to Méry proves it to me conclusively; but she acts it so well!" He knew moments of illusion in which Armance's perfect bliss finished by making him happy. "What other woman in the world," thought Octave, "even with more sincere feelings, could give me so much happiness?"

At last they had to part; no sooner was he aboard ship than Octave paid dearly for those moments of illusion. For several days he could no longer find within himself the courage to die. "I should be the least of men," he told himself, "and a coward in my own sight, if I did not, in accordance with the sentence passed upon me by the wise Dolier, quickly restore Armance her freedom. I am losing little in leaving this life," he added with a sigh; "if Armance acts the part of a lover so gracefully, it's no more than a reminiscence; she's remembering what she once used to feel for me. It would not have been long before I bored her. She probably esteems me, but no longer has any passionate feelings for me, and my death will distress her without driving her to despair." This cruel conviction in the end succeeded in making Octave forget the divine beauty of Armance intoxicated with happiness and *swooning* in his arms the night before his departure. His courage returned, and, by their third day at sea, with courage came back peace of mind. Abeam of the vessel was Corsica. The recollection of a great man so unhappy in death entered Octave's mind, and restored his resolve. As he thought of him unceasingly, he all but had him as a witness to his conduct. He feigned a deadly illness.

208

Fortunately the only officer of health available on board was an old carpenter who claimed some knowledge of fevers, and he was the first to be deceived by Octave's delirium and his horrifying condition. Thanks to a few moments of pretence, Octave could see after a week that they were despairing of his recovery. He sent for the captain in what they called one of his lucid spells, and dictated his will, which the nine members of the crew signed as witnesses.

Octave had taken care to deposit a similar will with a notary in Marseilles. All that he had at his disposal he left to his wife, on the extraordinary condition that she should remarry within twenty months of his decease. If Mme Octave de Malivert did not see fit to fulfil this condition, he begged his mother to accept his fortune.

After he had signed his will in the presence of the whole crew, Octave lapsed into great weakness and asked that prayers for the dying be said; some Italian sailors recited them beside him. He wrote to Armance, and enclosed with his letter the one he had found courage to write in a Paris café, and the letter to her friend Méry de Tersan which he had discovered in the orange-tree tub. Never had Octave been more under the spell of the tenderest love as in that supreme moment. Except for the manner of his dying, he granted himself the happiness of telling everything to his Armance. Octave languished on for more than a week, and each day he indulged in the new pleasure of writing to his beloved. He entrusted his letters to a number of sailors, who promised to take them personally to his notary in Marseilles.

A ship's boy in the crow's nest cried: "Land-ho!" It was the mainland of Greece and the mountains of Morea that were now visible on the horizon. A fresh breeze swept the ship briskly on. The name of Greece revived Octave's courage: "Land of heroes, I salute thee!" he murmured. And at midnight on the 3rd of March, as the moon rose behind Mount Kalos, a mixture of opium and digitalis prepared by himself gently released Octave from this life, which for him had been so restless. At daybreak he was found lifeless on the deck, lying across some coils of rope. There was a smile on his lips, and his rare beauty struck even the sailors who were ordered to bury him. The manner of his dying was suspected in France by none but Armance. Soon afterwards, the Marquis de Malivert having died, Armance and Mme de Malivert took the veil in the same convent.

TRANSLATORS' NOTE

ARMANCE was published in 1827. It may be apposite to outline the events which prompted Stendhal to venture for the first time into the medium of the novel; these events will perhaps give a measure of the delicacy with which he handled his theme, a theme revealed in his letter to Mérimée overleaf.

Mme la Duchesse de Duras, in 1825, was becoming known as a novelist specialising in socially outrageous themes, and her novel *Olivier or The Secret*, though unpublished, had been privately read to a few friends. Although treated with discretion, its subject became the talk of literary Paris, and a certain M. Hyacinthe de la Touche was moved to write and publish anonymously a novel called *Olivier*, which appeared at the beginning of 1826 in a form identical with that of Mme de Duras' earlier published novels. So clamant was the ensuing scandal that de la Touche was obliged to announce that he was not the author of *Olivier*, that he knew the author, and that it was not Mme de Duras. Shortly after the publication of *Olivier* Stendhal wrote a long review of the book for the *New Monthly Magazine*, in which he attributed it to Mme de Duras.

It was at the height of this literary tourney that Stendhal (who four years earlier had devoted a chapter of *Love* to the same subject) decided to enter the lists himself, and in January 1826 he began work on a fastidiously cryptic novel, revealing his theme only by naming his hero Olivier. But he later changed the name to Octave, thus placing the "secret" quite beyond the reach of the uninformed reader.

This translation is made from the text established by the late Henri Martineau and published by Editions Garnier Frères, Paris, 1950. Reference was also made to the text published by Editions Champion, Paris, 1925. The translators gratefully acknowledge the assistance of Mr. Lawrence Wood, and their indebtedness to M. Martineau's annotation.

S. & G. S.

LETTER FROM STENDHAL TO PROSPER MERIMEE ON THE SUBJECT OF ARMANCE

Paris, 23rd December 1826

IMPOTENCE IS more frequent than one would think. A woman whom you see on Mondays has an Olivier. In that charming little fragment of the *Memoirs of the Duchesse de Brancas*, published by the late Duc de Lauraguais—de Mareste will lend it to you—there are two impotents, to wit M. de Maurepas, minister, and M. le Marquis de La Tournelle, the first husband of the Duchesse de Châteauroux. I have also made a study of Swift in Sir Walter Scott's *Lives of the Novelists*.

I chose the name Olivier without any deep thought about it, because of the challenge. I favour it because this name alone is a disclosure, and a disclosure without indecency. If I were to put Edmond or Paul, many people would fail to guess the fact of *Babilanism* (an Italian word describing the case of M. Maurepas). I wish to create interest in Olivier, to give a true portrayal of Olivier. The dénouement you suggest, with Lord Seymour taken by surprise, etc., comes from the brain of a good dramatist, but ultimately my poor Olivier is odious. Wise people will say : "Hang it all, when one is a *babilan*, one doesn't marry ! Olivier comes to be a nuisance to his wife and Lord Seymour—away with him, and good riddance !" *Babilanism* leads to shyness; otherwise nothing better than to own up. That Monday's husband, M. de Maurepas, M. de La Tournelle all did it. M. de La Tournelle died in despair, and madly in love with his wife. Olivier, like all Babilans, is quite an expert

212

on the auxiliary methods in which *le Président* glories. A deft hand and an officious tongue would have given Armance keen sensations of pleasure. I am sure many girls have no precise notion what physical marriage consists of.

I am equally certain about this second and much more frequent case: the consummation of the marriage is repulsive to them for *three or four years,* particularly when they are tall, pale, slim, and blessed with a fashionable waistline. It's true that Armance is a copy, taken from the lady-companion of M. de Stroganoff's mistress, the one who was always at the Bouffes last year.

Like you, I have the strongest scruples about the letter written by the Commandeur. But I must have a little ground for stopping the confession. My experience has taught me that a modest girl much prefers to put her letters in a hiding-place than to hand them to her lover in person. She dares not even look at that lover when she knows he has just read the letter she has written.

Malivert is the name of my village; *Bonnivet* is the name of François I's favourite admiral. Had he had issue, Bonnivet would have been more or less like Montmorency, and better than Luynes and Sully.

This novel is too *erudito,* too learned. Has it enough warmth to keep a pretty French Marquise awake until two in the morning? *That is the question.* That was my feeling on receiving your letter. Mme d'Aumale is Madame de Castries whom I have made to behave. But reverting to the question of warmth, you say nothing about it. Is this a bad sign? If the novel is not of such a kind that it makes you burn the midnight oil, what's the use of writing it?

Would a young woman take an interest in Olivier?

I have a love-scene to write. Armance will say she is in love. Olivier would encroach upon the character of the *cuckold* if he were to kill himself because of this accident; the whole thing would relapse into another *Meinau,* as in *Misanthropie et*

Repentir.

The genuine Babilan must kill himself in order to avoid the embarrassment of making a confession. As for me (but at the age of forty-three years eleven months), I should make a beautiful confession, and I should be told : *What of it?* I should take my wife to Rome. There a handsome countryman, at a cost of one sequin, would pay her three compliments in one night.

But this truth is numbered among those which cannot be expressed by depiction *in black and white,* by depiction through the imagination of the beholder. How many true things are beyond the reach of art? For instance the love inspired by a man without arms or legs, like that vile creature who disgraces your office.

It seems to me therefore that the Babilan ought not to be a cuckold. Your supreme cuckold is *Emile,* who married for love and esteem. Have you read that sequel to *Emile? Dean Swift* wished not to marry in order to avoid making the confession; he did marry, entreated by his mistress, but never saw her *in private,* no more so afterwards than before.

In the drawing-room of a Comte, peer of France, of the nobility since 1500, and very wealthy, I am cold near the window when the North Wind blows. Your objection springs from *global truth,* my assertion from *a study of Nature.* Your objection would be perfectly sound in England.

I have re-read your letter :

Even though Armance, abed with my Olivier every night in Marseilles, were surprised :

(i) She adores him, and with his hand he gives her two or three ecstasies each night.

(ii) From shyness, from feminine modesty, she would not dare to say anything.

But love alone is enough to explain everything.

The kind of portrayal I am using, that of black upon white, does not permit me to pursue the truth. In 2826, if civilization continues and I come back to the Rue Duphot, I shall relate how Olivier bought himself a fine Portuguese *dildo* made of India rubber, which he attached to his own belt, and with which, after giving his wife one complete ecstasy, and another *almost complete* ecstasy, he bravely consummated his marriage in the Rue du Paradis, Marseilles.

When one is a dreamer, an intelligent man, a student at the Ecole Polytechnique, as Olivier was, that's what one does. Giving ecstasies with your hand—what an excellent euphemism to avoid the dirty word fr*g! Object of Olivier's meditations : giving ecstasies, etc., has been the object of Olivier's meditations throughout his youth. It is necessary you should know that he spent his youth frequenting wantons; it is this that I have tried modestly to convey. Armance recounts to him the slander which is being circulated concerning him.

But for God's sake reply on the question of *warmth*! Keep my letter, and perhaps we will talk about it again in 1828.

Comte DE CHADEVELLE